KING LEAR

– a novel –

PAUL ILLIDGE

Creber Monde

For Peter and Vicky Elmslie

Published by Creber Monde Entier
265 Port Union, 15-532
Toronto, ON M1C 4Z7 Canada
(416) 286-3988 1-866-631-4440 toll free
www.crebermonde.com
publisher@crebermonde.com

Distributed by Independent Publishers Group
814 North Franklin Street
Chicago, Illinois 60610 USA
(312) 337-0747 (312) 337-5985 fax
www.ipgbook.com
frontdesk@ipgbook.com

Design by Derek Chung Tiam Fook
Communications by JAG Business Services Inc.
Printed and bound in Canada by Hignell Book Printing, Winnipeg, Manitoba

First Printing August 2006

Library and Archives Canada Cataloguing in Publication

Illidge, Paul
King Lear : a novel / Paul Illidge.

(The Shakespeare novels)
ISBN 0-9686347-6-1

I. Shakespeare, William, 1564-1616. King Lear. II. Title.
III. Series: Illidge, Paul. Shakespeare novels.

PR2878.K7I45 2006   C813'.54   C2006-904408-2

KING LEAR

Text of the First Folio 1623

Characters

Lear	*King of Britain*
Goneril	*his eldest daughter*
Regan	*his second daughter*
Cordelia	*his youngest daughter*
Duke of Albany	*married to Goneril*
Duke of Cornwall	*married to Regan*
King of France	
Duke of Burgundy	
Earl of Kent	*adviser to Lear*
Earl of Gloucester	
Edgar	*his elder son*
Edmund	*his illegitimate younger son*
Fool	*attendant to Lear*
Oswald	*Goneril's steward*
Curan	*follower of Gloucester*
Old Man	*Gloucester's tenant*
Turlygod	*a mad beggar*

A herald, a captain, officers, a doctor, knights, soldiers, attendants, servants and messengers

As the power of the Druid wizards waned, the warrior Lear defeated the peoples of the south and west, from the boulder ruins at Stonehenge, to Ilfracombe on the Sea, thereafter ruling all Britain for the next forty years. Little is known of his young wife the Queen, but the story was told that she died during the birth of her third child, a daughter, who was given her mother's name: Cordelia.

The King Lear's eldest daughter, bold Goneril, held sway in her father's western reaches, with her husband, the revered Duke of Albany, while the second born, timid Regan, lived in the lands of the south with her husband, the ambitious Duke of Cornwall. Lear himself maintained a stronghold in the east, where armies from across the channel in France were expected to strike at any time.

Old and battle-worn, the King Lear had listened to his right hand power, the sagacious Earl of Kent, and after much deliberation had agreed with the wisdom of seeking a marriage between his youngest daughter, and a prince of France, in order to keep peace and stave off war with that country, which Lear could ill afford at his advanced age. Hence, the most eligible suitors had been invited to present themselves at the court of the British king, in hopes of gaining his youngest – and it was said his favorite – daughter's engagement. Cordelia, besides having her mother's name, was also held to possess that beauty of face and spirit by which King Lear, as a young man, had been smitten in his beloved Queen long ago.

The week preceding the betrothal day saw the King Lear's noblest subjects from all parts of the realm passing through towns and villages of the east as they made their way to the great gathering at Lear's castle. A royal banquet, the likes of which had never been known, would celebrate the friendship between the two kingdoms that had been foes for as long as anyone could remember....

In the Great Hall where Lear has ordered the royal feast to be held following Cordelia's betrothal ceremony, the Earl of Kent gives the King's chief steward some last-minute instructions then hastens over to the royal Fool, who is leaning against the large stone hearth in his parti-colored jester's costume and belled cap, eating an apple while he watches the enormous sides of beef and pork roasting on black iron spits over the crackling log fire, drips of fat hissing and sputtering every few seconds on the red-hot coals below.

Time to go, Kent plucks the apple from the Fool and, tossing it to one of the cooks, leads the slight little man toward the door, the small bells on his jester's hat jingling along with those on the curled toes of his slippers as he's led away, protesting through a mouthful of apple that he can walk very well on his own. But Kent, whom the King has put in charge of organizing events on this most important of days, is all business and refuses to loosen his grip until they're outside the Great Hall, where he dispatches the Fool to fetch the King straightaway from his chamber, while he proceeds in a different direction, toward the Throne Room. Striding briskly along a few moments later, Kent is looking down rather than ahead when he rounds a corner into the adjoining corridor and, as a result, bumps into the elderly Earl of Gloucester, a friend of the King's since childhood days who is late arriving from his domains in the south-east. Pleased to see each other, they exchange apologies and friendly greetings, Kent taking Gloucester kindly by the arm as he explains to the ageing earl that there's no time to lose: the ceremony is about to begin.

Before they have gone far, Gloucester, long concerned about the question of succession, puts the issue before his friend.

"As one with the King's ear, what is your opinion of these changes he's proposed, my lord Kent?"

Kent offers a genial shrug. "I had always thought he preferred Albany to Cornwall."

"It seemed so to me as well," Gloucester nods, his eyes narrowing to a frown, "but now that he has decided to divide up the kingdom – I've heard he has such equal regard for them both he cannot in fairness favor one over the other – " Walking faster than he should be, Gloucester soon has to stop and catch his breath, at which point a young man who has been following them comes to stand with the two earls.

Kent smiles. "Is this not your son, my lord?"

"His upbringing has been my responsibility, sir," Gloucester says, "a fact which I've had to acknowledge so often over the years that I'm rather brazened to it now."

"I'm not sure I conceive – "

"Well, sir, this young fellow's mother could," Gloucester chuckles and resumes walking, "whereupon she grew round in the belly and nine months later had a son for her cradle before she had a husband for her bed. A shame, really."

"I wouldn't say that, sir, the result being so proper," Kent says admiringly.

"But I *do* have a legitimate son, sir," Gloucester quickly adds, "several years older than this lad, yet I can assure you he stands not a jot higher in my estimation for all that. You see, though this rascal came eagerly into the world before he was sent for – his mother was fair indeed and some good sport was had at his making, I can tell you – yet someone had to be his father," Gloucester confesses. "Do you know this noble gentleman, Edmund?"

"No, my lord."

"My lord of Kent: remember him in future as an honorable friend."

"Your obedient and humble servant," Edmund says, offering a respectful nod.

"We must talk further so I may come to know you better," Kent says amiably as they arrive at the Throne Room doors.

"I will endeavor to make your efforts worthwhile, sir."

Kent smiles and lets Gloucester and Edmund precede him.

"He's been abroad the last nine years," Gloucester hurries to explain, "and he'll be going away again soon – " But he's forced to break off since Kent has signaled the guards to close the doors.

Moving inside, Kent leads Gloucester and Edmund through the ranks of assembled lords, nobles and knights to the very front of the room and onto the dais, Gloucester bringing Edmund with him to his appointed place among the realm's most notable earls, majestic in their long robes and noble regalia, while Kent hastens forward to his position immediately to the right of the throne.

"The King is coming," Gloucester whispers to his son, pointing toward an open door at the side of the room where, following a regal trumpet fanfare, the royal party makes its entrance led by a one-eyed soldier in full battle armor, solemnly carrying a purple cushion in his hands on which a small, gold crown has been placed. Behind him comes King Lear, despite his age a formidable presence still: his white-haired head defiantly erect above his broad shoulders, his eyes dark-ocean blue, his white beard long and untrimmed now that his fighting days are over. He mounts the dais and moves to the throne but remains standing as Goneril and Regan, wearing gold crowns like the one being borne on the purple cushion, take their place to his left with their husbands, the dukes Albany and Cornwall, while their younger sister Cordelia stations herself across from them, between the crown-bearing soldier and Kent, who throws a disapproving frown at the Fool, sitting cross-legged and comfortable on the floor alongside the throne, casually inspecting a fresh apple of which he's preparing to take a bite.

Lear turns to Gloucester. "Wait with the lords of France and Burgundy until we are ready."

"I shall, my lord." Bowing, the aged earl makes his way off the dais and goes out.

"Meantime, we shall reveal reveal the purpose for which we have gathered you before us… Give me the map there," he commands. Two scribes step forward and unfurl a parchment scroll before him, showing the kingdom of Britain. Lear gazes out at the expectant faces of his devoted subjects, most of whom have served no other monarch in more than forty years. "Know," he declares with firm authority, "that this day we have divided in three our kingdom, and with our advancing age are fast resolved to shake all cares and business off these weary shoulders, passing them now to younger strengths, so, thus relieved, we may crawl unburdened toward our death." He nods at his daughters' two husbands. "Our son of Cornwall, and you, our no less deserving son of Albany, we are this hour determined to disclose our daughters' separate dowries, that strife tomorrow might be prevented by making known today what will be theirs at my demise. As well, the two great princes, France and Burgundy, strong rivals for our youngest daughter's love, have lingered long with us at court in hopes that each will win her hand, which choice we will make known today as well. Tell me, my daughters – since now we are relinquishing our power, land and cares of state – which of you shall we say loves us most, that we the largest portion of our bounty may bestow on her whose affection merits it the most. – Goneril, our eldest, speak first."

Goneril curtsies and begins to speak. "Sir, I do love you more than words can ever tell: more precious than eyesight, liberty and freedom, in ways beyond all value, rich or rare, no less than life itself, than honor, grace and beauty – as much as any child ever loved, or father found, my love takes breath away and betters any words. Beyond all manner of things, this is how I love you."

Astonished by her sister's speech, Cordelia turns away. "What shall I say?" she wonders to herself. "Love, and keep silent…"

Pleased, Lear sweeps his arm over a sizeable portion of the map. "Of all within these boundaries, from this line," he points, "over to this, with ancient woods and pastures rich, with plentiful rivers and meadows green, we make you queen. To your and Albany's descendants, be this in perpetuity."

Eyebrows raised, the Fool glances up at Kent, who is clearly uneasy.

" – What says our second daughter, our dearest Regan, wife of Cornwall? Speak."

Regan steps forward and curtsies before the King. "Sir, though I am of the same mind as my sister, and in my heart do feel the words she speaks are what my love is too, I find her falling short, for I confess myself an enemy to all other joys and find I am only happy in your dear highness's love."

Cordelia turns aside once more. "The worse this is for Cordelia. And yet perhaps not, since I am sure my love's more true than words in speech."

With a gratified smile, Lear points to another section of the map and answers Regan. "To you and yours, for all time," he pronounces, "be this ample third of our fair kingdom, no less in size, worth and pleasant aspect than that conferred on Goneril." Regan bows her head and returns to stand beside Cornwall, who smiles discreetly. "– But now our joy," Lear begins in a warmer voice, "our last but in no way our least, for whose young love the lords of France and Burgundy contend – in hopes of being allied to us in blood and power – what can you say to draw a third of the kingdom more opulent than your sisters'? Speak."

Cordelia hesitates, aware that all eyes are upon her. "Nothing."

For a moment, Lear's gaze remains the same.

"Nothing?" he asks, as though there might be some confusion on her part.

"Nothing," she says again.

"Nothing will come of nothing," he says quickly, "speak again."

"Unhappily for me I cannot just put the feelings of my heart so suddenly into words, as others do. I love Your Majesty as I think a daughter should, no more and no less."

"Now, Cordelia, mind your words," Lear grumbles, "lest they affect your fortunes here."

"So please you my lord, you have bred me, raised me, loved me. I return those duties back to you as are right and fit, which is to say I obey you, love you and most honor you. Why do my sisters have husbands if, as they claim, they love you above all? I hope when I am wed, that lord whose hand I take will carry half my love with him, half my care and half of what I honor. I shall certainly never marry, as my sisters have, and love my father more than he who is my husband."

"And goes your heart along with this?" Lear asks, perturbed.

"Yes, my good lord."

"So young yet so unkind?"

"So young, my lord, and true."

The room in hushed silence, Lear moves from behind the map and crosses to confront his daughter, an aggravated stare in his eyes. Undaunted, Cordelia meets them with her own.

"It shall be so!" he fumes. "Let truth be your dowry then, for by the sacred radiance of the sun," he curses, "the mysteries of darkness and damnation – by the power of the stars that shape the course of human fortune, I here disown you as my flesh and blood, and hold you banished from my heart, and me, forever. The barbarous savage who kills his young to stuff his gorge shall now be closer to my heart, my pity and my aid, than you, who once was my daughter."

"Good, my lord – " Kent protests.

"Quiet, Kent. Come not between the dragon and his wrath. I loved her most, and set my comfort in old age upon her loving kindness. Get out and avoid my sight!" he rails at Cordelia. "Let me die in peace alone – " he raises a fist and shakes it fiercely in her face, "as here I tear a father's heart from his wounded chest!" Turning from her, he storms toward the throne. "Call France. Go!" he yells in livid anger, but no one on the dais dares move. "Call France and Burgundy!" he cries again, several attendants rushing terrified from the room. Breathing hard, Lear glares at the map of his kingdom. "Cornwall and Albany, with my first two daughters' dowries, take now this other third. Let pride," he sneers bitterly, "which she calls 'plain speaking', seek her hand in marriage. "As of this moment I turn my power, pre-eminence and privileges of kingship over to you both. We, in the course of each month, with a hundred knights retained as is my right, will reside with each of you in turn. Only my title shall I maintain, and all honor due a king: the rights of rule and reign, along with all else, will be yours henceforth, my beloved sons. Which to confirm – " He steps toward the one-eyed soldier and takes the small crown off its cushion. " – I give you this to share between you."

"Royal Lear," Kent speaks up, "whom I have honored all my life as King, loved as my own father, followed as my master, as my patron have included in my prayers – "

"The bow is bent and drawn – beware its arrow."

"Let it fly, though it strikes me in the heart: Kent is left no choice when Lear is mad. What has come over you, old man? Forbidding me to do my duty when I see power taken in by flattery? Honor itself demands I speak out when majesty stoops to folly. Do not divest yourself of royal power – think what will come from such a rash and reckless deed. I'll stake my life your youngest daughter does not love you least, nor are those without feeling whose words aren't what we hope to hear."

"Kent, if you value your life, no more."

"My life's only value is serving and defending my King. I've never feared to lose it – your royal life has always mattered most to me."

"Out of my sight!"

"See better, Lear," Kent bristles, seizing him by the arm, "or let me die standing in your way."

"By Apollo – " he threatens and shakes off Kent's grip.

"By Apollo, King, you swear to your gods in vain – "

"Insolent wretch!" Lear bursts and moves to draw his sword.

"Don't, sir!" Cornwall and Albany protest, restraining him.

"Do!" Kent fumes defiantly, daring Lear to strike him. "Kill your physician and blame it on this illness now infecting you! Take back your kingdom," he clamors, "or while this voice within me can say, I'll tell thee you do wrong to give it away!"

"Hear me, traitor!" Lear thunders in reply. "On pain of death, hear me! Since you seek to have us break a vow we've made – which we have never done in all our years – and with haughty pride have dared to question our decree, which neither our person nor our place can bear, my powers in effect, let the price of broken obedience be this: you have five days to ready yourself with belongings and provisions. On the sixth day you will have turned your back on this our kingdom for good. If by the tenth day your banished person be found in our domains, you will be slain where you stand. Away! By Jupiter, this shall *not* be revoked."

"Then farewell, my King," Lear says after a moment. "If this is how things are to be, freedom lies elsewhere for one like me. My leave I gladly take from thee." He turns to Cordelia. "The gods keep you in their sheltering kindness, maid," he says fondly, "not just for thinking so, but having spoken rightly. And your lofty speeches," he says with a look to her sisters, "may your deeds prove them true, and right things follow these loving words from you."

He takes off the gold chain and medallion he wears around his neck, but Lear only looks away, and no one in the royal party moves to accept it from him. The bells on his cap jingling in the awkward silence, the Fool shakes his head *No!*

"Thus Kent, O Princes, bids you all adieu. He'll make his old way, in a country new." He tucks the chain medallion inside his robe, bows to the King, and has just departed when trumpets sound, signaling the entrance of Gloucester with the heir to the French throne and the Duke of Burgundy, each followed by a richly dressed entourage of noble young men, attendants and servants.

"The Princes of France and Burgundy," Gloucester announces and returns to his place beside Edmund.

"My lord of Burgundy," Lear says, seating himself on the throne, "I will address you first, who along with France has sought our daughter's hand. Tell me, what is the least you would require in present dowry – which not being received, you would cease your quest for love?"

"Most Royal Majesty, I expect but what Your Highness has declared to me."

"Right noble Burgundy," he explains, "when she was dear to us we held her of precious value. But now her price has fallen. There she stands, sir. If you see something in what little she has to offer – anything which is fit to your liking – and with our having cast her off as well, but having, I remind you, nothing more in this world: there she is, all yours."

"I know not how to answer, my lord," Burgundy says uneasily.

Lear continues, impatiently. "With these imperfections she possesses, being friendless, cursed, hated, and without dowry, a sworn enemy to us now – will you take her or leave her, sir?"

"I beg your pardon, Majesty," Burgundy defers, "but I see not how a choice can come from me, when all is changed from what you promised previously."

"Then don't take her, sir," Lear comes back quickly, "for by the power that made me I've told you what wealth remains to her." He shifts his eyes to the second French suitor. "As for you, great King, I would not strain our friendship so far as to have you accept what is hateful to me, therefore I beseech you to turn your affections toward one more worthy of them than a wretch who Nature herself is now ashamed to acknowledge as one of her own."

France steps forward and bows before Lear. "It is strange that she who until now was loved most, who was the subject of highest praise, deemed the comfort of your old age – your best and dearest child – should in such brief time have done something monstrous enough to strip her so entirely of your favor, my lord. Surely her offence must be so horrible in nature that it can't be forgiven, or else she was not worthy of your avowed affection in the first place, which, as I have come to know Cordelia, reason would not allow me to believe was true."

Heartened by France's words, Cordelia turns to her father. "Though I lack the glib and oily art of those who make promises they have no intention of keeping, and because I don't boast of what I will do until it has been done, I must beseech Your Majesty that you make known the fact it is no vicious deed, no murderous evil, no disgraceful action nor shameful conduct that has deprived me of your grace and favor, but only something which is not in me to say, and because of which I feel myself a better person: I look to win no favors for myself through flattering words, though not having them has lost me your love."

"Better you had never been born than not to have pleased me better," he says and, with a reproachful sneer, turns away.

"Is it only this?" France asks, " – her reluctance to speak of things she does not feel?" He glances at Burgundy. "What are your intentions toward this lady, sir? Love cannot be love when it is tied to considerations that have naught to do with matters of the heart. Will you take her?" he asks, his eyes returning to Cordelia. "She is a dowry in herself."

"Royal King," Burgundy says, moving to Cordelia's side, "if you are prepared to give that dowry of which we first spoke, then here I take Cordelia's hand – " he does so, "as Duchess of Burgundy."

Lear keeps his eyes trained in front of him. "Nothing. I have sworn. I will not change."

"I am sorry then," Burgundy apologizes to Cordelia, "that in losing a father you must also lose a husband."

"Peace be with Burgundy," Cordelia answers graciously. "Since wealth and fortune concern him so, I could never be a true and loving wife to him."

"Fairest Cordelia," France says tenderly, "who is most rich although poor, most desirable although forsaken, most loved although despised, you and your many virtues I here do gladly seize upon. If it be lawful, I take up what's been cast away. Gods, gods," he remarks for all to hear, " – it is strange that despite your cold neglect, my love should kindle to inflamed respect. Your dowerless daughter, King, thrown to me by chance, is queen to us, to ours and our fair France. Not all the wealth of treasured Burgundy could buy this spurned and yet so precious maid from me. Bid them farewell, Cordelia, though they've been unkind: what's lost here, in a better place you will find – "

"You have her France," Lear announces and rises from his throne. "Let her be yours, for we have no such daughter nor shall ever see that face of hers again. Therefore be gone, without our grace, our love, our blessing. Come, noble Burgundy!" he calls, and sweeping his robes around him makes a hurried departure, his entourage of nobles, knights and attendants moving quickly to keep up behind.

When the last of the assembled guests have left the room, Cornwall passes the small crown that would have been Cordelia's, to Albany, who on his way out hands it to his wife Goneril. Feeling the eyes of the Fool on her, she gives him a contemptuous look. He only glares, first at the jeweled crown she wears on her head then the small gold one she holds in her hand. The enmity between them almost palpable, he joins Gloucester a moment later, Edmund lingering after his flustered father has gone to bow before Goneril and Regan, who remain behind in the now empty room with their younger sister and the King of France.

"Bid them farewell, Cordelia," he says gently and stands quietly by her side as she glances at her sisters.

"The jewels of our father…" she says pointedly, looking from one to the other. "With tearful eyes Cordelia leaves you." Goneril, an indifferent expression on her face, avoids Cordelia's eyes altogether, while Regan reaches over and takes the small crown in her hands, admiring it with a self-satisfied smile on her face that is clearly designed to annoy her younger sister. "I know what you are," Cordelia continues calmly, "yet because I am your sister I will keep myself from putting into words those accusations as to what you've done. Love our father well. To your vaunted affections I leave him. And yet," she worries, "alas, if only I were still within his grace, I would prefer to see him in some other place. But things being what they are, I bid farewell to you both."

"Do not tell us what to do," Regan comes back. "Let your concern be to please your husband, who in charity agreed to take your hand." France glowers but keeps respectfully silent. "You have a daughter's obedience willfully neglected, and for that, you are deservedly rejected."

"Time will bring to light what cunning is here employed," she warns, "and those of devious purpose, in the end will be destroyed. Prosper well, my sisters."

"Come, my fair Cordelia," France says to break the ensuing silence. He turns to leave, then waits for Cordelia to join him and they go out together.

Suddenly agitated, Goneril leaves off brooding and seizes the gold crown Regan has been holding. "Sister, there is much we need to talk about. I think our father is planning his departure for tonight."

"It's most certain he is, and to live with you – next month with Cornwall and me."

"You see what age is doing to him?" she asks and shakes her head. "He changes his mind from one minute to the next – he always loved our younger sister most, and casting her off as he has done, but shows how poor his judgment has become."

"It's the weakness of old age," Regan agrees, "though he has always known himself too little."

"He's been like this throughout his life: rash, impatient, wanting things his way. The ailments and complaints of age but harden habits long ingrained."

"More impulsive whims are bound to follow then, as this the banishing of Kent…"

Goneril nods. "There are still the formal courtesies to be observed before the King of France departs," she says uneasily, " – pray you, sister, let's agree one with the other: if our father goes on wielding power in such a vexing state of mind, his giving up the throne like this, can only bring us harm."

Regan places her hands over Goneril's on the gold crown. "We should plan for ourselves without delay."

Goneril meets her sister's eyes. "Strike while the iron is hot, I say…."

High atop the Earl of Gloucester's castle tower, flags are snapping in the heavily gusting wind as bad weather moves in from the east. Edmund, sitting on a stone bench at the foot of the flagpole, looks up from a letter he is writing and gazes out at the approaching storm, the wind blowing his long hair back from his face…

"You are the goddess I worship, Nature. I abide by your law and no other. Why in minding custom and tradition should I allow a mere and petty distinction deprive me of fair fortune and my father's title, simply because I was born some twelve or thirteen months after my brother?"

The first drops of rain hitting his face, he goes back to writing and quickly finishes, moving his pen in practice strokes above the letter before he signs. Shielding the paper from the rain with his body, he sprinkles drying sand from a shaker but it flies right off the paper in the wind, so he blows on the ink for a moment then folds the letter and slips it in a brown leather pouch that hangs from the sword belt around his waist.

"Why bastard?" he shouts, turning into the wind. "Why 'lowly bastard', when *my* qualities are as fine, *my* mind as apt and ready, *my* person as legitimate as any mother's child could ever be? Why brand *me* as low? As being *lowly*? The *lowest*? A lowly *bastard*? Low? Bastard? Here's to *bastards*!" He hurls his inkpot at the battlement so it shatters against the stone wall in a burst of broken glass and wet, black ink.

The rain falling harder now, Edmund hurries across the roof platform and goes down a set of stairs, through a small wooden door at the bottom and along a tunnel passage that soon widens into a corridor proper.

"Bastards…" he mutters as he walks, " – who in the lusty stealth of their hearts have more passion and desire than ever would be found by night within a dull, stale and tired marriage bed, where none but simpering fools are bred. Well then *legitimate* Edgar, I will have your lands and title. Our father's love is as great toward the bastard Edmund as it is to *legitimate* Edgar. Fine word 'legitimate.' Well, my legitimate," he gloats, "with what I have in mind to do – and with this letter cleverly placed – *lowly* Edmund will see the 'legitimate' disgraced!"

He reaches the bottom of a narrow, winding staircase and proceeds along an archway, stopping part way to peer between the stone columns into an open atrium below: his father, shaking his head in consternation, is handing back some letters and a pair of spectacles to a servant who is standing with him.

Edmund stays out of sight, leaning his head back on one of the columns. "Thus I rise," he says, "and thus succeed." He takes out his letter, brings it to his lips and kisses it. "Now you gods," he smiles on his way to the stairs at the end of the archway, "stand up for bastards…"

Alone in the atrium, Gloucester is worried.

"Kent banished? France departed in anger? The King no longer on the throne, his power in other hands? And all this done so suddenly – " He breaks off when he notices his son coming toward him, engrossed in a letter he's reading. "Edmund!"

Glancing up at the sound of his name, Edmund acts surprised to see his father and immediately whisks the letter out of sight.

"How now Edmund, what's the news?"

"So please your lordship, none," Edmund says, shrugging.

"Why were you so eager to put that letter away?"

"I have no news, my lord."

"What was it you were reading?" Gloucester frowns.

"Nothing, my lord."

"Then why put it away in such a hurry? For goodness' sake, there's no reason to hide it if it was nothing. Let me see," Gloucester persists, but Edmund shakes his head in refusal. "Come now, if it's nothing then I won't need my spectacles."

"Forgive me, sir, but I can't. It's a letter from my brother that I haven't finished reading, and as for what I've perused so far, I don't believe it's fit for your eyes."

"Give me the letter, sir," Gloucester demands.

"I'll be in the wrong whether I give it or not, but it's the contents that are to blame, at least as I understand them."

"Let's see, let's see," his father pesters until Edmund reaches inside his cloak.

"I hope for my brother's sake he wrote this but to test me," he protests and hands over the letter.

Gloucester opens it and reads: "'This policy of reverence for old age makes the world a bitter place for those of us in the prime of life. It keeps our fortunes from us till we ourselves are too old to enjoy them. I've begun to feel like a slave in bondage to this oppressive tyranny of old age, which wields power over our lives only because we allow it to. Meet with me so that I may tell you more. If our father were to sleep and never waken, you would enjoy half his revenue for ever, and remain the beloved of your brother, Edgar.' Hum!" he exclaims in shocked disbelief. "Conspiracy? 'Sleep and never waken…enjoy half his revenues.' My son Edgar!" he cries. "Had he a hand that could write this? A heart and brain to conceive of such a thing? When did you receive it? Who brought it to you?"

"That's what is unusual, my lord. It was not brought to me, it was thrown through the window of my room."

Gloucester studies the letter. "Is this your brother's writing?"

"If what he had written were to the good, I would swear it was his. But with what's written here, I can't see how it could be."

"It is his."

"It is in his handwriting, my lord, but I hope his heart is not in the contents."

"Has he ever sounded you out about this?"

Edmund shakes his head. "Never, my lord. Though I have from time to time heard him suggest that it is only fitting, when sons reach their maturity and fathers enter their twilight years, the father should be looked after by his sons and the sons manage their revenue – "

"O villain, villain!" Gloucester howls, outraged. "The very opinion he expresses in this letter! Abhorrent villain, unnatural, detested, savage villain – worse than savage! Go, sir, and seek him out. I'll have him arrested. Abominable villain! Where is he?"

"I'm not certain, my lord. If it would please you to restrain your indignation against him until you can discern more clearly what his intentions really are, you would be much safer than if you chose a violent course of action when you may have mistaken his purpose. That would be a serious breach of honor and shatter his respect for you. I would stake my life on the fact that he wrote this only to see what my feelings were toward you, not for the purpose of doing you harm."

"Do you think so?"

Edmund nods. "If your honor finds it acceptable, I could place you in a position where you could hear us talk of this, so you can judge what he says for yourself, and it could easily be done by this evening."

"He can't be such a monster."

"Nor is he, surely."

"To feel this way about his father who so dearly and completely loves him," Gloucester protests. "Heaven and earth!" He reflects for a moment. "Edmund, find him if you would and see if you can gain his confidence. Frame the matter according to your own discretion. I would give up my very earldom to know the truth…"

"I will seek him at once, sir, and pursue this business further. As soon as I can, I will let you know our next step."

Reassured, Gloucester begins to pace. "These recent eclipses of the sun and moon do not bode well for us," he declares solemnly.

"Though the wisdom of science can explain things this way or that, the world finds itself punished with the consequences nonetheless: love cools, friends are suddenly estranged, brothers become enemies to each other. In cities there is rioting, countries descend into discord, in palaces treason comes to the fore, and the bonds between child and parent are split asunder. The villainous behavior of my own son attests to this: a disgruntled child pits himself against his loving father." He hands the letter back to Edmund, shaking his bowed head. "Even the King veers from the natural course of things – there's father against child, as I told you. No, Edmund, our best days are behind us," he laments. "Conspiracy, duplicity, treachery and all manner of havoc are sure to plague us to the grave…" He sighs wearily, but then turns abruptly toward his son. "Confront this villain, Edmund. You will lose nothing by it. Just…do it with care," he urges. Content with Edmund's nod that he will, Gloucester starts to walk away, stopping after only a few steps. "And the noble, true-hearted Kent banished for his honesty," he says with his back to Edmund. "Most strange," he murmurs to himself and, after a moment, carries on across the room.

Edmund stares after his father, watching as he reaches a wooden door in the far wall, the struggle to open it almost proving too much for his thin, old arms.

"Such is the foolishness of the world," Edmund sneers as soon as his father is gone, "that when we're troubled and unhappy, often from the excesses of our own behavior, we blame the sun, the moon and the stars: as if we were villains by the dictates of destiny, fools by heavenly determination, thieves, thugs and traitors by the alignment of the stars on the day we were born; drunkards, liars, adulterers because the circling planets made us so – and everything about us that is evil the sole and necessary result of some divine decree! A pat excuse for the lecherous man," he says with disdain, "to point up a life's lascivious ways as no fault of his own, but of his stars. Puh! My father and mother conceived me under Aries and I was born under Taurus, so does it follow that I am a ram-like, bear of a man? Rubbish! I would have been what I am had the sweetest, most serene star in the sky twinkled on my bastardizing – " He hears someone coming and glances behind to see Edgar making his way toward the atrium. "With what apt timing he comes," Edmund grins, "the helpless dupe in a comedy farce. My cue – " he strikes a pose of great concentration that his brother will notice, "shall be woeful melancholy, with plaintive cries like the long-suffering lunatic: *O these eclipses – we're doomed to strife and disharmony! Mi, fah, so, la – BAH!*" he shrieks wildly as Edgar comes to stand with him.

"Good day, brother Edmund, what are you in such serious contemplation of?" he inquires with sarcasm, amused by his brother's theatrics.

Playing the madman, Edmund squints his eyes in hostile suspicion, hesitating briefly before he speaks: "I am thinking, brother, of a prediction I read the other day as to what these eclipses will leave in their wake."

"Do you busy yourself with that sort of thing?" Edgar asks lightly.

"I promise you," Edmund says ominously, "this man's predictions of misfortune always come true." He begins to talk faster, his voice anxious and distressed. "Feuds within families, famine and death, the dissolving of lifelong friendships, the country divided against itself, threats and curses about the King and his nobles, needless betrayal, banishment of friends, desertion of allies, marriages torn apart…and I know not what else – " he finishes quickly, gasps and starts coughing because he's rushed to deliver the words in a single breath.

"Since when have you believed in astrology?" Edgar asks wryly.

"Never mind," Edmund snaps, switching back to his normal voice. He quickly pulls Edgar behind a nearby column. "When did you last see our father?"

Edmund makes a face. "Why, the night just gone by."

"Did you talk to him?"

Edgar nods, confused. "For two hours we were together."

"Did you part on good terms? Did he act as if you had said or done something to upset him?"

"Not at all."

"*Think*, if you can," Edmund persists, "how you might have offended him. And let me warn you: stay away from him for a while, at least until his wrath has cooled, which at the moment is raging so fiercely that even an injury to you would not appease his present anger."

"Someone has done me wrong," Edgar protests.

"That's what I'm afraid of," Edmund agrees. "However, patience and self-restraint are what's needed most right now. I suggest you keep to yourself until the worst of his rage has passed. You can stay in my chamber if you like, and when the time is right I will take you to a place where you can hear my lord speak. Get going. Here's my key." He nudges Edgar to start moving then abruptly brings him back "If you do come out for any reason, I pray you, go armed."

"Armed, brother?"

"Edgar, I tell you, for your own sake go armed." He glances warily about the atrium, speaking in a hushed whisper. "I would be dishonest if I said there were no ill feelings toward you now. I've told you all I've seen and heard – but even that is no true picture of the awful truth. I pray you, get going," he urges and sends Edgar on his way.

"Shall I hear from you soon?" he calls back.

Edmund nods in assurance. "I am yours to count on, brother!"

A brief and grateful wave, then Edgar moves hastily through the atrium and is gone.

Pleased with himself, Edmund's lips curl to become a gloating smile. "A gullible father and an unwitting brother, whose nature so forbids him from doing harm that he suspects none – against whose foolish honesty my plot succeeds with perfect ease. I know what must be done. I will, if not by birth, have lands by using my wits. And all with me is fair in this, so long as Edmund benefits…" As he starts walking, he lets out a joyful yelp and, to amuse himself, recites in a mocking voice the list of predictions he gave Edgar: "Feuds within families a country divided," he races through the list, "desertion of allies threats and curses banished nobles needless betrayal famine and death dissolving of friendships marriages torn…*BAH!*"

While King Lear and his hundred knights are out hunting, their squires, servants and attendants are busy in the large encampment of tents spread across the field in front of Goneril's and Albany's stone-towered castle. Slanting rays of late-afternoon summer sun bathing the weathered walls in gold, some of the servants bear buckets of water, bales of hay and armloads of firewood from inside the castle out to their camp, while others lug the carcasses of deer and wild boar, killed in the morning hunt, into the castle kitchens to be roasted and fed to King Lear and his royal retinue during their nightly hunting feast.

Looking peeved, Oswald, the castle's chief steward, is keeping a careful eye on the comings and goings from his position beside the open castle gate, when a servant informs him that Goneril, a look of livid anger on her face, is marching through the inner yard on her way outside the castle.

Without entourage or attendants, she pushes past her father's retainers, spots Oswald and makes her way over to stand with him, acknowledging his bow with a curt wave of her hand and getting straight to the point.

"Is it true my father struck you for scolding his Fool?"

He points to a sore-looking red welt on the side of his face. "Yes, madam."

"Day and night he insults me! Every hour he flies into a violent rage over one thing or another, which sets us all at odds. His knights are boorish and unruly, and he himself takes me severely to task on none but trifling matters."

She waits while he goes over to a wagon leaving the castle that has stopped halfway through the gate, the rustics sitting atop its load of hay, playfully pitch-forking small bits at the servants who are heading into the castle carrying empty water buckets.

Oswald speaks sternly to the wagon driver, who scowls and curses at him before clicking the reins to start his wagon moving again. But as Oswald turns to go back to Goneril, a whole forkful of hay lands on his head and cascades over his shoulders then down the front of his steward's uniform. Outraged, yet wanting to save face, he lets the offence go and returns to Goneril, who is fuming now.

"I'll not endure this any longer," she says sharply. "When he returns from hunting I will not speak with him. Say I am sick. As well, hold back on those duties he has come to expect from you. I'll accept the blame for any slackening myself – "

The sound of hunting horns goes up in the distant fields

"I hear him returning, madam," Oswald says, looking uneasy. Goneril gazes resentfully at the sprawling encampment that occupies the land in front of her castle: badly put up tents, makeshift stables, messy latrines. "Put on what lazy negligence you please, you and your fellows," she says sternly. "I will broach this matter with him. If he dislikes it, let him go to my sister, who happens to be of one mind with me: we will be over-ruled by him no more." She reflects a moment. "Foolish old man," she says scornfully, "thinking he yet wields that power which he has given away." She meets Oswald's eyes. "When idle old fools become misbehaving children again," she advises, "they must be treated with firm scolding and humored with coddling words. Keep that in mind."

"Very well, madam."

"And let his knights have cold looks from all of you," she continues, "never mind what comes of it. Advise the servants so. I want this to come to a head, and it shall, so I may confront him about these disgraceful goings on. I'll write my sister straightaway to follow this same course. Come, prepare for dinner."

She turns and precedes him through the gate, neither of them glancing back as the hunting horns blare once again, the frenzied baying of the King's hounds barely audible over the sound of thundering hooves as Lear and his hundred companion knights gallop toward the castle for dinner....

In a far corner of the King's encampment, the banished adviser Kent stands alone between two tents at the end of a long row. Dressed like a common peasant now, his hair cut short in spiky tufts and crude patches, he is griming his face with a mixture of black ashes and lamp oil.

"If I can but disguise my way of speaking to go along with my now changed appearance,' he says to himself, "then I may well achieve my purpose." He sets down the grime mixture, plucks a shirt from the pile of clothes at his feet, rubbing and wiping his face with it until the skin has a dark and weathered look. "Now, banished Kent, if you can pass yourself off to the very man who condemned you, it may come about that your own revered master will hire you to work for him again." Briefly amused, he grows quickly serious, bundles the rest of his clothes together and, taking up his walking staff, steps out from between the tents. Making his way through the deserted camp, he soon spots what he's looking for: smoke from a burning fire. He hurries over and, after glancing around to make sure no one is watching, tosses the clothes he wore in his former life onto the flames. His face solemn as he watches them burn, he stirs the fire with the end of his staff until a small blaze begins, then turns and starts along a cart path in the direction of the hunters' horns, which are sounding again…

There's considerable commotion outside the castle gate when the hunting party rides up, horns continuing to blow, hounds barking, an army of squires, grooms and servants rushing to attend to the knights as they dismount from their panting horses, laughing and hollering ribald jokes at their companions while heading to the castle entrance where Lear waits for them to assemble.

"Let me not be kept waiting for dinner," he warns one of his knights. "Go and see that it's ready." He watches as the knight promptly departs, his eyes then drawn to an unusual looking man staring at him from a short distance away. "You there," Lear calls, "who are you?"

"A working man, sir," Kent answers in a strange accent.

"What do you profess yourself to be? – And what would you have with us?"

"I profess to be no less than I seem, and I would like to serve that man who will have confidence in me, who I can look up to as honest, who is wise and patient. I value justice, I fight when I have no other choice, and I say my prayers."

Lear moves closer and peers suspiciously at Kent's face. "Who are you?"

"A good and honest-hearted fellow, and as poor as the King,"

Kent says without flinching.

"If you're as poor for a subject, as he is for a king, you're poor, that's certain," he jokes and the knights crowding around him burst into laughter. "So, what is it you want, sir?"

"To be of service."

"Service to whom?"

"You."

"Do you know who I am?"

"No sir, but you have that in your face which makes me want to call you master."

"And what would that be?"

"Authority, sir."

Lear ponders the remark a moment. "Of what service could you be to me?"

"I ride well and run swiftly, I can tell pretence from honest affection, hold secrets in confidence, and I deliver the plain truth bluntly. In short I am qualified to do anything an ordinary man is fit for, and my best trait is perseverance."

"How old are you?" Lear inquires.

"Not so young to love a woman for her character, nor so old that I would play the doting fool to her every whim. These legs have carried me through forty-eight years, sir."

"Very well," Lear says. "You shall serve me for now. If I like you no less after dinner I will hang onto you a bit longer." Kent acknowledges Lear's decision with a bow of his head and falls in behind the knights as Lear raises another shout for "Dinner!" and points his boisterous throng of followers toward the gate. "Where's my boy, my Fool?" he demands of a knight walking at his side. "Go, find him and bring him here."

The knight hurrying off as ordered, he passes Oswald, waiting nearby for the King to notice him.

"You! You sir!" Lear calls to him. "Where's my daughter?"

"Never mind, so please you," Oswald mutters, then turns and walks away.

"What says the fellow?" Lear cries and abruptly dispatches another knight. "Call the blockhead back! Where's my Fool?" he yells impatiently as he prepares to deal with Oswald. "I think the world's asleep..." he complains.

The knight sent to fetch Oswald returns without him.

"Well, where's that insolent dog?"

"He says, my lord, your daughter is not well."

"Why came he not back when I called him?"

"Sir, he answered me most rudely, and said he would not."

"Would *not*?" Lear bellows.

"My lord," the knight offers, "I know not his reason, but in my opinion Your Highness is not being treated with that same respect for courtesy and custom you were before. There's a marked lessening of both among the servants in general and, it appears, in the Duke and in your daughter herself."

"Herself? You think that?" He glares at the knight.

"I beg your pardon if I am mistaken about this, my lord, but duty forbids me to keep silent when I see Your Highness being wronged."

"No," Lear shakes his head, "it but confirms my own sense of things. I've perceived a faint neglect of late, but wondered if this was my own suspicious nature more than a deliberate attempt to shun me." He broods for a brief moment. "I will look further into it. But where's my Fool? I've not seen him these last few days."

"He's been pining sadly since your youngest daughter's departure for France, sir."

Lear looks thoughtfully away. "No more about that, I've noted it," he says, quickly dismissing the subject. "You!" he snaps at one of his knights, "go and tell my daughter I would speak with her." He gestures to another. "And you, go bring me my Fool!" The knight rushing off, Oswald has reappeared and deliberately placed himself in Lear's line of sight.

"O you, sir! You! Come here sir!" Lear barks at him.

A brazen look on his face, Oswald meets Lear's eyes but doesn't move. Lear stalks over and confronts him, his rowdier knights crowding up behind.

"Who am I, sir?" Lear demands.

"My lady's father."

"My lady's father?" Lear looks around at his men with a

menacing scowl. "You, your lord's lackey," he erupts, "you dreg, you slave, you cur!!"

"Begging your pardon," Oswald objects, "I am none of these things, my lord."

"You dare dispute with me, you wretch?" Lear takes his horse crop and lands several vicious blows on Oswald's head before he can put up his hands to protect himself.

"I'll not be struck this way, my lord!" he cries, backing away toward Kent, who puts out his foot.

"Nor tripped neither, you oaf?"

Oswald stumbles on Kent's outstretched leg and falls to the ground, Lear's knights roaring with laughter.

"I thank thee, fellow," Lear smiles at Kent. "You serve me thus and I'll make of you a friend."

"Come, sir," Kent warns Oswald, "on your feet." He grabs Oswald roughly under the arms and stands him up. "That will teach you respect for your betters. Go on," he says, and shoves Oswald. "Get going, unless you care to be knocked down again, you blundering dolt. Away!" A look of desperation on his face, Oswald would like nothing better than to leave, except that several knights are having fun blocking the way each time he takes a step. "Get moving if you know what's good for you!" Kent teases. He puts the end of his staff in Oswald's back and shoves him on his way, the embattled steward squeezing between the two knights, who give way only after a final bit of jostling. A pathetic figure, Oswald flees for the castle gate amid resounding jeers and catcalls.

"Well, my trusty fellow," Lear says, addressing Kent, "much thanks." He takes out a coin. "There's something for your efforts." Kent catches the silver piece and pockets it.

" – Let him work for me too," the Fool quips and with his jester's hat in hand, the hair on his bare head in short braids strung with dozens of small seashells, he scurries past the King over to Kent and holds out his fool's cap.

"My good lad, how is it with you?"

Looking up at Kent, the Fool ignores Lear's question.

"Seriously, sir," he insists with Kent, "you'd better take this." He shakes his cap so the bells jingle.

Kent makes a face. "Why, Fool?"

"Why? For taking the part of one who's fallen out of favor! If you can't see which way the wind's blowing," he says with a warning wink, "you'll soon catch cold. So there," he says, pressing the hat on Kent, who reluctantly accepts it. "And beware: this fellow here – " he points to Lear, "has banished two of his daughters and given the third his tender blessing, but against his own will – if you follow him, believe me, sir, you'll be needing this more than I." He leaves the cap with Kent and comes back to stand with Lear. "How now, Nuncle?" He makes a mocking-sad face. "If only I had two fool's caps and two daughters," he apologizes.

"Why, my boy?"

"Well, if I gave them all I had, I would at least have two caps for myself. Here's mine I could give you…" He whistles and snaps his thumbs for Kent to toss back his hat, which he does, then despite Lear's resistance, tries placing the cap on the King's head. Finally he stops, heaves a pitying sigh. "Now you will have to beg one from your loving Daughters," he says.

"Take heed, sir, the whip," Lear frowns and makes a threatening gesture with his horse crop.

The Fool smiles knowingly. "Truth's a dog been sent to the kennel," he taunts, "driven out to make room for the flattering bitch that's taken its place…"

"A festering sore, nothing more," Lear grumbles.

"Oh sir," the Fool shakes his head as though gravely disappointed, "I'd best teach you a speech then."

"Do."

"Pay attention, Nuncle." He strikes a pose beside Lear and holds up a finger with each phrase: "Hide more than you show…speak less than you know…ride more than you go…lend less than you owe…reap just what you sow." He continues with the fingers of his other hand. "Believe more than you pray for, bet less than you play for, avoid drinking and whores, stay often indoors, and you shall have more – " he wiggles all ten fingers in Lear's face, " – than two tens in a score."

"This is nothing, Fool," Kent scoffs.

The Fool shrugs. "We get what we pay for," he comes back, "you gave me nothing for it."

"Come, boy, nothing can be made out of nothing," Lear protests.

Holding a hand in front of his mouth, the Fool appeals to Kent. "I pray you, sir, remind him that's as much as he got for his land. He won't believe it if a fool tells him."

"A sharp fool," Lear gripes and finally turns to head into the castle, his hundred-strong train of knights traipsing across the castle yard behind him, the Fool and Kent.

"Do you know the difference, my boy, between a sharp fool and a dull one?" the Fool asks while they walk through the castle yard.

"No lad, tell me."

"The man that counseled you to give away your land…" He runs in front of the King and holds up a hand for the procession to stop, which it does, though Lear is not amused. "Place *that* fellow here by me," he puts his arm around an imaginary man's shoulder, "while *you*, for him, go there and stand." He points to a spot beside Lear, but the King, spotting a door up ahead, walks impatiently around the Fool.

"The sharp and dull fools will presently appear!" the Fool shouts after Lear for all in the castle yard to hear, "the one in fool's clothes here," he indicates himself, "the other, much like a royal king, he hurries to finish, "charging for the door over there!"

With no one to open the door for him, Lear stops and turns. "Are you calling me a fool, boy?" he bristles.

Several knights rush forward to get the door, even though it is too small and non-descript to be anything more than a servant's entrance.

" – All your other titles you have given away," the Fool remarks nonchalantly, strolling forward to confront the King, "even that you were born with…" he snipes accusingly, and bows as Lear, disgruntled, steps inside.

"This is not fooling, my lord," Kent objects once they're in the castle, Lear leading his throng through an impossibly narrow hallway just off the kitchen: cooks, attendants and servants too busy with dinner preparations to take notice of the imperial presence until they catch sight of the knights streaming in behind.

" – No, indeed it isn't," the Fool agrees, "lords and great ones will *have that from me no more!*" he says in a mocking tone. Scurrying to keep up with the King, he shakes his head in confusion. "Indeed, if I had the monopoly on fooling," he reasons, "they'd receive a healthy share for all they do. And the ladies, sir," the Fool stays right behind the King, "they, of course, won't let me keep the fooling for myself, and like the lords and great ones, they've started doing it too," he chides.

Unable to make way and bow as the King comes by, the servants crowding through the halls continue about their business, Lear at one point having to wait while a hapless servant works frantically on his hands and knees to clean up the basket of garden vegetables he's dropped on the floor in all the commotion. The Fool offers to hold a bowl of brown eggs for another servant standing nearby so he can get down and help the first before there's trouble: all can feel Lear's temper mounting "Nuncle," the Fool says to ease the King's growing frustration, "you give me an egg and I'll give you two crowns." He holds out the bowl full of eggs.

"Two crowns. How so," the King grumbles, picks out an egg and tosses it at the Fool, who motions Kent forward to hold the eggs while he continues. "After I've cracked the egg in two – " He quickly does so. "And swallow what's inside – " He plops the yolk in his mouth, swallows and holds up the half shells. "Two crowns! When you split your crown in two, and gave away both parts," he pitches the empty shells over his shoulder, "you were like that fool, tricked in the fable, who carried his ass through the mud, instead of *it* bearing him: Sir, you had little wisdom in that crown of yours when you gave the golden one away – let anyone be whipped who tells this Fool it isn't so!" he rails.

Lear, cantankerous and unwilling to wait any longer, barges ahead down the corridor, one of his legs knocking the just-refilled vegetable basket as he goes, but with the King's rowdy knights pushing forward en masse, the servants can only watch in helpless chagrin as the vegetables are squashed and flattened by their trampling boots.

Scurrying after Lear, the Fool starts up with a bitter, mocking song: "*Fools have ne'er been treated with less grace* – " With no idea where he's going, Lear heads up the first staircase he comes to. " – *For wise men grown foolish take their place,*" the Fool sings on the stairs, " – *knowing not how their wit to share, and their manners? A perfect disgrace!*"

"Since when were you so full of song?" Lear asks as he reaches a landing and stops to catch his breath.

"It's been my practice since you made your daughters your mothers," the Fool explains, mimicking Lear's gasps beside him on the landing. Lear takes his horse whip when he realizes the Fool is mocking him, and pokes him in the side.

"The whip…" he threatens.

"For when you pulled down your pants and gave them your scepter," the Fool says and glances below Lear's waist, "you let them take your manhood too." He makes a pitying face. "*'Then they for sudden joy did weep, and I for sorrow sung: that such a king should play Bo-Peep, renounce his throne, and go the sheep among.'*"

The crowd of knights pushing up from below, Lear moves to open a door on the landing. The Fool stops his hand. "I pray you, Nuncle," he pleads, meeting Lear's eyes with an earnest look, "hire a schoolmaster who can teach your fool to lie. I would gladly learn how to lie…"

"You lie, sir," Lear threatens, "and we're sure to have you whipped." He opens the door and goes through into a wide, curving hallway.

"I wonder how thee and thy daughters should all be so alike," the Fool says, watching as the King decides on a direction to take. " – They'll have me whipped for telling the truth, you'll have me whipped for lying, though now that I think, sometimes I am whipped for holding my piece…"

Lear leaves him and trudges off, the Fool running to keep up but turning around so he's walking backwards, facing the King. "I'd rather be anything than a fool," he muses, "and yet I wouldn't be *you*, Nuncle. *You've* pared your wisdom on both sides and left nothing in the middle – " He halts suddenly and motions for the King to look behind him. " – Here comes one of the parings now."

Goneril comes toward her father, but the door from downstairs opens, Kent and the hundred knights flooding into the hall around her, anger reddening her face.

"How now, daughter," Lear mutters warily, "why that frowning look? Methinks there's been too much frowning of late…" Walking back down the hall, his knights make way in respectful silence as he passes.

"You were a fine-looking fellow," the Fool pipes up, "when you had no need to worry about her frowns." He shakes his head sadly. "Now you are but an 'O' without a number. I am more than you are now." He ponders the thought. "I am a fool, you are nothing." He turns to face Goneril, who throws him a disdainful look.

"No, no," he puts up his hands in protest, "I will hold my tongue. Your face bids me do so, though the words you say are none. Not even mum!" he winks, "mum's the word!" he whispers. "*'He that leaves the crusts on his bread,'*" he sings, "*'shall want them one day before he's dead.'*" He points a blaming finger at the King. "There's the pea, its shell removed – "

Goneril turns to her father. "Not only *this* your all-disrupting fool," she scolds, "but others of your insolent crowd do shout and argue hour upon hour until their tempers burst and they erupt in gross displays of riotous and not to be endured behavior. Sir, I had assumed that in making this known to you before, the problem would be dealt with, but I now grow fearful that by things which you yourself have recently said and done, you defend them in their behavior, turning blind eyes to its very going on. If this is the case, and you continue to encourage them against my will, I shall take matters into my own hands, for the good of all, and though it may embarrass or offend you, I will be thought right in doing so."

"Beware, Nuncle," the Fool warns. "The sparrow tended the cuckoo's brood. But the birds grew up, and one day ate the sparrow for food. *Phht!* Then out went the candle, and all were left confused!"

Enraged, Lear levels his eyes at Goneril. "Are you our daughter?" he sneers.

"Come, sir," she answers lightly, "I wish you would make use of that good wisdom which I know you possess and forego these angry moods which drive you from your right mind."

The Fool purses his lips and frowns. "Even an ass can tell when the cart begins to pull the horse. Whoop, Jug!" He smiles and claps his hands, "I love thee!"

The King turns to his knights crowded together up and down the hall, Kent among them, a worried look on his dark, grimed face. "Do any here know me?" Lear shouts and begins pacing before his men. "Why, this is not Lear. Does Lear walk like this? Does Lear talk like this? Where are his eyes? Either his mind is going or his faculties are asleep – Ha! Am I awake? I can't be. Who is it that can tell me who I am?"

"Lear's shadow," the Fool puts in mischievously.

" – I would like to know, for by all the trappings of sovereignty, by the powers of logic and reason, I could be tricked into believing I had daughters."

"Who will make obedient fathers," the Fool quips.

Lear glares bitterly at his daughter. "Your name, fair lady?"

"Sir, this pretending to be amazed at what I've told you is no different than any other of your recent pranks. I do beseech you to understand me clearly: as you are old and well revered, you should behave accordingly. Here you keep a hundred knights and squires, men so coarse, unruly and debauched that this our castle, infected with their utter lack of manners, begins to seem a wild and bawdy inn. Their pleasure-seeking gluttony and lust, make this our gracious home seem more a tavern or a brothel, than a palace. This shameful state of things requiring instant remedy, you are requested by her, who if ignored will see that what she asks for shall be done, to reduce the size of your train somewhat: have those you retain to attend upon you be men who befit your age, who know themselves, and you."

"Darkness and devils!" Lear cries and storms away. "Saddle my horses! Let my knights make ready!" He wheels and returns to Goneril. "Degenerate bastard," he swears at her, "I'll burden thee no more. I have another daughter."

" – You strike my people and your disorderly rabble treat their betters as though they were servants!"

" – Take back what you said to me, before it is too late!"

Goneril turns her head away and waits as her husband Albany appears in the hall and comes to stand with her. Lear turns on him immediately. "O, sir," he sneers, "is this your feeling too?"

"I pray you, sir, be patient," Albany says uncertainly.

" – Prepare my horses!" Several knights bow to the order and depart. "Ingratitude, you cold-hearted fiend," Lear resumes with Goneril, "is more horrible from a child, the rending pain so deep – " When she appears to be ignoring him, he explodes: "Defaming lies! You detestable *kite*! My train are men of excellence and accomplishment, well versed in all particulars of duty, and strict in their regard for all that honor does require of them!" His words hang emptily in the air, Goneril still refusing to look at him. Albany glances uneasily at the Fool, who rolls his eyes in jest, then frowns.

Lear stands alone in the middle of the hall. "O little seeming fault in Cordelia," he murmurs to himself, "and yet it shook my feelings to their foundation, drained my heart of all its love, made matters much the worse." He looks down. "O Lear, Lear, Lear," he scolds himself, "beat at this head that let foolishness in and precious reason out." He glances up. "Go, go my people!" he waves for his knights to disperse, and they do so, crowding toward the door through which they entered.

"My lord, I am guiltless as I am ignorant of what has moved you," Albany says quite sincerely and comes over to Lear, who meets his eyes.

"That may be so, my lord. That may be so." He walks back and stands in front of Goneril and waits till she looks at him. "Hear, Nature," he curses, "hear dear goddess, hear: withhold thy bounty if though didst ever intend to make this creature fruitful. Into her womb convey sterility, dry up in her the organs of birth, that never from her body spring a babe to honor her. If Destiny will have her breed, let her be delivered of a child of malice, that may from birth to age a cruel and spiteful torment be. May it carve upon her youthful face such lines of hurt and pain that tears wear channels in her cheeks as down her face they fall. Turn all her mother's kindness and labor to laughter and contempt, that she may feel how sharper than a serpent's tooth it is to have a thankless child. Away," he declares furiously, "AWAY!!"

Lear shoves past those of his knights still remaining in the hall and practically flings himself out the door, Kent and the Fool moving fast to follow right behind…

Perplexed, Albany appeals to Goneril. "By the gods that look down upon us, why does he act this way?"

"Don't trouble yourself to know more," she replies, "it's but the bitter mood of old age and a failing mind." She turns to leave, but Lear – Kent and the Fool a step behind – rushes back into the hall and confronts her.

"What means this, that *fifty* of my followers must be gone within a fortnight?" he cries indignantly.

"What's the matter, sir?" Albany falters.

Lear glowers, close to tears. "I'll tell you," he says resentfully, standing so he's eye to eye with Goneril, who regards him indifferently. "Life and death, I am *ashamed* you have the power to strip me of my manhood thus – " he wipes his eyes with an unsteady hand, " – that these hot tears, which come against my will, should make you worthy of them; plague and sickness upon you! The deepest, never-healing wounds of a father's hateful curse pierce every sense within you, and, foolish old eyes," he laments, "if ever you weep like this again I'll pluck you out and cast you with your tears into the sea for fish to eat. Has it come to this?" he demands of his daughter. "Has it?" Goneril blatantly ignores him. "Then let it be so! I have another daughter who I'm sure will be kind and comfort me: when she does hear of this her nails will tear your wolfish eyes from your head! You will find that I'll resume the shape you think I have cast off for ever," he warns, his voice cracking. "You will see, I promise you." He wheels around and once more makes his exit through the hall door, Kent holding it open for him, and then they are gone.

Goneril smirks in the ensuing silence and then turns to her husband.

"Do you hear that, my lord?"

Albany shakes his head in consternation. "Though my love should have me take your side, Goneril, I cannot – "

"Content yourself that he's gone," she remarks sharply. "Oswald, come here!" she calls, noticing out of the corner of her eye that the Fool has lingered a little distance away. " – You, sir, more scoundrel than fool," she says dismissively, "after your master."

"Nuncle Lear, Nuncle Lear, wait and take the fool with thee!" he pleads mockingly and fixes Goneril with a sarcastic look, backing along the hall toward the door. "A fox when her husband caught her," he taunts, "to her father such a daughter," he frowns, "sent him to the slaughter," he points an accusing finger, "noosed him by his old gray head," he mimes a rope going round his neck, "his poor fool hung right after!" he makes a choking sound, yanking on the imaginary rope so his tongue slips out the side of his mouth as he staggers along the hall and out the door.

Goneril turns to Albany. "Someone has given the old man wise counsel – a hundred armored knights at his disposal!" She scowls and shakes her head. "Yes, so that every impulse, desire or whim he can indulge with a hundred soldiers to see that he gets his way? While our lives are held at mercy? Oswald, I say!" she calls impatiently.

"Well," Albany offers, "you may worry too much."

"Better than not enough," she comes back stiffly. "I'd rather be rid of those I fear than have them be rid of me. I know what's in his heart. I've written my sister about what transpired here. If she receives him and his hundred knights after I have shown his unfitness – "

Oswald arrives and presents himself.

"Here, madam."

"How now, sir, have you written the letter to my sister?"

"Yes, madam."

"Take some others and ride to her immediately. Inform her of my concerns and add reasons of your own why something must be done. Be on your way, and return with haste.

When Oswald has gone she continues with Albany. "No, no, my lord," she reproaches him, "this meek and gentle way of yours, though I condemn it not, yet you are more apt to be blamed for want of wisdom than praised for your excessive mildness."

He studies her face a moment. "How far those eyes may pierce I cannot tell, but striving to make things better we often harm what's well."

"No, if he – "

"Time will tell," he suggests, cutting her off, then turns and walks away, Goneril, displeased, watching him uneasily as he goes….

1.5

Evening is coming on outside Goneril's castle. The gate has been closed on King Lear and his knights, who are packing up to move. Tents and other shelters in the encampment have been taken down, servants and attendants are loading trunks, equipment and provisions onto a long line of baggage carts, and the horses, resisting their bridles after a long day on the hunt, are being made ready, but not without difficulty.

Squatting in front of the only fire still burning, the Fool is holding a roasting stick over the coals in an effort to finish cooking a small piece of meat before it's time to go. King Lear is beside him on a campstool, giving Kent instructions.

"Take this letter on ahead to Gloucester. If my daughter or others inquire about its purpose, say you are not privy to the contents." He hands over a sealed letter which Kent slips under his cloak.

"I will not rest, my lord, until it is delivered." He bows and hurries off through the encampment.

Shifting the roasting stick's position, the Fool notices Lear staring into the fire.

"If a man's brains were in his feet," he wonders, "would his thoughts feel the cold?"

"I suppose."

"Be merry then. Yours will stay warm."

"Ha, ha, ha," Lear laughs.

"You'll see your other daughter will treat you kindly, for though she's as like this one as a crab's like a crabapple, yet I can tell what I can tell."

"And what's that, my boy?"

"She will taste as much like this one as a crabapple tastes like a crab."

Lear grunts, amused.

"Take the nose. Can you tell why it stands in the middle of one's face?"

"No."

"Why, to keep one's eyes apart, so that what a man cannot smell at least he can see."

Lear ponders a moment. "I did her wrong," he says absently.

"Can you tell how an oyster makes his shell?"

"No."

"Nor I neither. But I can tell why a snail has his shell."

"Why?"

"Why, to protect his crown," he says and taps a finger to his head, "not to give it away to his daughters."

"I will forget that I am her father," Lear decides. "And such a kind one too," he adds, turning from the fire. "Where be my horses?" he calls to a party of grooms lugging saddles over to the stabling area.

"Your asses are getting them," the Fool says, poking fun. He pulls his stick away from the fire and licks his lips while inspecting the brown morsel of roast meat. "The reason why the Seven Stars are no more than seven is an excellent reason," he poses.

"Because they are not eight?"

"Yes indeed," the Fool grins, "you'd make a good fool."

"To take it away by force – the ingratitude!"

The Fool glances over, shaking his head. "If you were *my* fool, Nuncle, I'd have you beaten for being old before your time."

"Why is that?"

"You shouldn't have grown old without becoming wise." Deciding the meat is ready for eating, he offers the roasting stick to Lear.

"O let me not be mad," Lear says in his distraction. "Not mad, sweet heaven. I must not be mad." He looks to the Fool. "Keep me from madness…" "The horses are ready, my lord!" one of the grooms runs up and announces.

Lear takes the roasting stick and gets to his feet. "Come boy!" he calls and turns to go, turning back the next moment to toss the stick on the fire. The Fool panics and reaches out for it – but Lear pulls his hand back at the last moment, winks and hands over the roasting stick, the Fool chuckling now at Lear's jest.

They make their way over to the waiting horses, the Fool relishing his bit of meat as he scampers along beside the King.

"She may be laughing now as we take to our heels," he reminds Lear, "but worry not, Nuncle: laughter hides more than it ever reveals…"

1.5

King Lear mounting up, several grooms help the Fool onto the saddle behind him and they move off, the Fool playfully urging speed with taps of his roasting stick on Lear's back....

Night having fallen, torches are burning along the hall in Gloucester's castle where Edmund is pacing restlessly at the foot of a staircase that rises to a landing above. Peering up, he's suddenly aware of someone standing behind him. He turns quickly and sees it's one of his father's right hand men.

"Curran. Good evening."

"The same to you, sir. I have just been with your father and informed him that the Duke of Cornwall and Princess Regan will be arriving soon."

"How comes that?"

"I know not, sir. Although," he looks about to make sure they're alone, "you've doubtless heard the whispered news? The rumors, I mean, for as yet that's all they are…"

"Rumors?" asks Edmund.

"You haven't heard of an impending war between the two Dukes, Cornwall and Albany?"

"Not a word."

"You may hear before long then," Curran suggests, and turns to leave. "Farewell, sir."

Edmund watches him go, his words hanging ominously in the air. "The Duke and Regan coming here tonight – so much the better for me! The best!" he smiles, light from the flames of a nearby torch flickering brightly in his eyes. "Nothing could fit so well into my plans," he rejoices. "My father's guards are ready to seize my brother, and there is but this final piece of business I must do. May swift action and good fortune bring me just reward!" He turns back to watching the stairs, but has no sooner done so than his brother Edgar passes by the upstairs landing. "Brother, a word!" he calls and rushes over. "Come down, brother, I beg you!"

Edgar descends, Edmund seizing him by the arm the moment he reaches the bottom of the stairs and rushing him away in the torch-lit hall toward a dark alcove, talking with frantic urgency as they move along. " – Father is up in arms and has his men looking for you. You must flee, Edgar. He knows where you've been hiding. If you go now you will have the cover of night." Edgar tries to speak but Edmund cuts him off. " – Did you say something to offend the Duke of Cornwall? He's on his way here *now*, in great haste, *tonight*, and the Princess Regan with him. Are you *certain* you didn't take his side in the rivalry between him and Albany? *Think!*" he demands, pushing his brother against the alcove wall.

"No," Edgar falters, "I haven't said a word – "

Edmund leans out and scans the hall. "I hear them coming!" He takes out his sword. "Sorry brother, but I have to draw my blade so it looks – draw yours as if you're defending yourself. And fight your hardest against me!" He raises Edgar's sword and begins swinging his own so Edgar has no choice but to protect himself. "Surrender!" Edmund yells as he clashes harder with his brother. "Give yourself up! Light over here! Light I say!" Streaking across the hall, he takes down a torch, comes back and gives it to Edgar. "Hurry, brother, hurry!" he pleads and pushes Edgar to go.

Voices and shouts going up as Gloucester and his search party get closer, Edgar wavers in confusion.

"Torches, torches!!" Edmund hollers at the approaching search party then turns. "Farewell then," he says to Edgar and motions frantically for him to flee. "Go!"

Desperate and frightened now, Edgar realizes the danger he's in and departs running, the flame from his torch disappearing quickly down the hall…

Panting excitedly, Edmund flings himself against the alcove wall. "Some blood on me will make it seem I fought fiercely – " He takes his sword and with no hesitation runs the blade across his upper arm, his eyes closed, his teeth clenched against the pain. " – I"ve seen drunkards do worse than this for sport," he winces stoically, sets his sword in the shadows on the floor behind him and glances along the hall: Gloucester and his party of armed guards and torch-bearing servants are charging forward. Assuming a suffering pose, he waits until they've gone past then staggers from the alcove, calling in anguish: "Father, father, stop... Stop!" he moans desperately. "Someone – help me!" Stumbling and reeling badly, as if he's near collapse, he clutches the wounded arm against his chest, blood pouring profusely between his fingers as he lurches toward Gloucester. When he sees his father starting back, Edmund deliberately slows his movements and stretches out his good arm in an appeal for help, disappointment showing briefly in his stricken face as Gloucester, pre-occupied, appears to ignore his son's plight.

"Now, Edmund," he barks, "where's the villain?"

"He waited for me, here in the dark," Edmund explains breathlessly, "he had his weapon out and ready, he was chanting strange spells and asking the moon to look with blessed favor on the dreadful act – "

"Where *is* he?" Gloucester repeats.

"Look, sir, I bleed," Edmund groans, takes his blood-covered hand away from the wound and shows Gloucester.

"Edmund, where is the *villain*?" Gloucester persists.

"Fled that way, sir," Edmund says hoarsely, pointing with his good hand nowhere near where Edgar went, " – fled to the staircase yonder when he could by no means – "

"After him!" Gloucester yells to his men. "He went up there!" He turns back to Edmund. "When he could by no means *what*?"

"Talk me into killing your lordship – in spite of my telling him the gods would unleash their fury with a vengeance on one who murdered his father, and though I also reminded him of the dear and strong bonds between a child and its father. In the end, sir," Edmund gasps in mounting pain, "seeing how bitterly opposed I was to the unspeakable act he was bent on committing, with a cruel swing of his ready sword he lunged at my defenseless person, lacerating my arm, as you can see. Then, when he noted the courage with which I was resisting and pleading for someone to help me in my righteous cause, either startled by my bravery or stunned by the noise my shouts were making, he suddenly turned and fled."

"Let him fly where he may," Gloucester blusters, "but nowhere in this land can he escape being captured or caught – and killed... Noble Cornwall, my worthy patron and protector, will be here presently. By his authority I will have it proclaimed that any man who helps us bring this murderous coward to the stake, shall receive generous thanks, he who conceals him, death!"

"I pleaded for him to change his mind," Edmund tries to explain, "but he was so bent on doing murder that when I threatened to reveal his plot he cursed me and reviled me: 'You low and worthless thing,' he scoffed, 'do you really think your words would carry credence over mine, that any would believe a thing you said or find you could be trustworthy or true? No. I could deny everything – and I would, even if you found yourself with evidence in writing – I'd put the blame on you, the whole sordid plot, the scheming, the treachery. And you'd have to think the world most utterly stupid not to know the benefit that would fall to you, upon my death, provides the perfect motive for you to seek it.'"

"A heinous, calculating villain," Gloucester says in condemnation, "and he denied the letter was his, you say?" Edmund nods. "He is no longer a son of mine – "

Trumpets sound in another part of the castle signaling the arrival of visitors.

"That will be Cornwall," Gloucester says, frowning uneasily. "I am unclear why he comes," he mutters and ponders a moment before returning to the matter at hand. "I'll have all ships barred from sailing, the villain shall not escape," he assures Edmund, "the Duke will grant me that I am sure. Besides, a picture of his face I will have posted far and wide that all within the kingdom may note him as a wanted man. And of my lands, loyal and natural boy, I'll find the means to make you heir.

The search party that had gone after Edgar returns without him but they are heading the newly arrived Cornwall, Regan and their accompanying attendants along the hall toward Gloucester, who has offered Edmund his shoulder while they walk.

"How is it with you, my noble friend?" Cornwall asks, concerned. "When I arrived just now I heard the distressing news."

"If it be true," Regan allows, "all vengeance will be too little for such an offender. How are you my lord?" Gloucester steps away from Edmund to accept her greeting kiss.

"O madam," he laments, my old heart is broken, quite broken."

"Did my father's godson indeed try to kill you? He who my father named Edgar himself?"

"It's too shameful for words, madam," Gloucester mourns.

Regan reflects a moment. "Was he not a companion to the riotous knights attending my father?"

"I know not, madam. It is just too bad, too, too bad."

"Yes, madam," Edmund speaks up, "he was of that group."

"It's not surprising, then, if he was so disposed to doing you harm. They will have put him up to it, the murder of his father, no doubt to have his revenues for themselves. I have heard much about them this night, from my sister," she explains, "who warned that, should they come to me, it would be best for them to find me not at home."

"Nor I neither," Cornwall adds and turns to Edmund. "I hear you've done your father a son's devoted duty."

"I did what I felt I must, sir," Edmund replies modestly.

"He made known the plot to me and was wounded striving to apprehend his brother," Gloucester declares proudly.

"Is he being sought for?" Cornwall asks.

Gloucester darts a glance at the chief guard, who nods. "As we speak, my lord," he assures Cornwall.

"With his capture you shall no longer have cause to fear him, my power is at your disposal to use however you please. – As for you, Edmund, whose virtue and loyalty so commend you in our eyes, you are one with us hereafter. Natures of such deep and trusted quality we much will need." He clasps Edmund's hand and embraces him. "We welcome you with us," he smiles.

"I shall serve you, sir, in every way I can."

"I thank you, your grace, on his behalf," says Gloucester, elated that his son has been afforded such favor.

"But still, you know not why we come…" Cornwall says.

"And at this time of night," Regan adds then becomes serious. "Matters of great cause, noble Gloucester," she explains, "in which we have need for advice. Our father has written to us, and so has our sister, of disagreements between them which are better dealt with away from home, it seems to us. Their messengers are waiting now for our reply." She takes Gloucester's hands in hers. "Our dear old friend, take comfort if you can and know that your wayward son will feel our justice soon, yet meantime lend us your wisdom in this business between my father and my sister, to which we must give our utmost and immediate attention."

"I am at your service, madam," he assures her. "Your graces are most welcome here with me."

Cornwall motions for Gloucester to join him and they start back along the hall, Regan, walking with Edmund, drawn to the almost casual way he uses his teeth to tear a strip of cloth from his shirt, wrap it around his upper arm and twist the ends to form a tourniquet that will stop the flow of blood from his wound.

He glances up and smiles when he notices she's watching him. Their eyes meet for a moment, Regan offering a smile of her own before she looks away….

Kent and the King's men who have ridden with him are sitting on the ground inside Gloucester's castle yard watching without interest as Regan's and Cornwall's escort troops continue their night arrival: armed soldiers climbing down from their horses by the light of dozens of torches Gloucester's servants are holding up for them. Talking quietly among themselves, they gather and greet each other then head quickly into the castle, grooms leading their horses promptly off to the stables so that soon, with the disappearance of the servants back inside, the only light is from the full moon rising overhead. Weary and uncomfortable, Kent sighs quietly and closes his eyes, but no sooner has he done so than a door flies open down the way and two men come running from the castle. The men sitting with Kent jump to their feet and begin cheering for the man fleeing – one of Lear's men also – while they holler and boo his pursuer: a servant of Gloucester's who wields a dangerous looking meat cleaver…

The man in flight streaks toward Kent and the King's men, who band together and restrain the angry servant while allowing their man through. He comes over to Kent and lifts his cloak for all to see the two freshly roasted chickens and good-sized jug of cider he's procured. The servant curses and demands the food and drink be returned to the kitchen *at once*, sending up a threatening wave with his cleaver to emphasize the point.

" – Good evening friends," a voice beckons from close by, "would you be of this house?" Kent turns to see Oswald and eight of Goneril's soldiers sitting on their horses in the moonlight.

"We would," he says sourly. Standing in the shadow of the castle wall, he knows Goneril's steward can't see his face.

"Thiev – " the servant with the cleaver begins to shout but a firm hand quickly clamps his mouth shut. "Where may we put our horses then?" Oswald asks.

"In the dung heap."

"Some respect if you please," Oswald admonishes him.

"I've no respect for you, nor any desire to please you," says Kent.

"I beg your pardon," Oswald says stiffly, "but I don't care to be treated this way."

"What, like mongrel scruff? If I came upon a mutt like you in the pound I'd make you care soon enough."

"You have no cause to be impertinent, fellow. I know thee not."

"But I know thee."

"I somehow doubt that," Oswald says with a patronizing chuckle and the others of his party join in. " – You're a boot-licking lackey," Kent blurts, "a presumptuous vain and status-seeking nobody, a pompous cowardly nit-picking pander who arranges that others fight his battles for him, you have nothing to offer anyone but your haughty ignorant and worthless self and are no more in this world than the son and heir of a mangy mongrel bitch – one whom I will beat into a miserable whining pulp if you dare deny that a single syllable of what I've said is true." During his tirade he has made his way over to Oswald.

"You horrible, undignified man," Oswald sneers, "how dare you address me thus when you have no idea who I am, nor I you."

"Liar!" Kent shrieks, and in one swift movement reaches up and yanks him from his horse, the King's men whistling and cheering as Oswald tumbles to the ground. "Wasn't it just two days ago that I tripped you up and beat you before the King?" Kent demands, stalking Oswald as he scrambles on his hands and knees to get away. "Draw, you worthless sot! It may be dark but the moon is full!" Kent clamors, taking out his sword and walloping Oswald on the behind. "I'll poke holes in you till the light streams through – draw, you mincing minion! Draw!"

"Stay away from me," Oswald cries, back on his feet now but cornered against the castle wall. "I'll have nothing to do with you!"

"Draw, you conniving pawn," Kent says, closing in. "You come with letters against the King! Draw your sword and fight or I'll carve you like a piece of meat – draw, you rogue!" He plants several warning blows on Oswald's legs.

"Help here!" Oswald cries to Goneril's men, but they have chosen to hang back in fear of Kent's raging temper. "Murder, help!" Oswald pleads pitifully, his arms up in front of his face.

"Take out your sword and fight!" Kent shouts furiously. "Fight, man!" He inflicts more harmless blows, the King's men boisterously mocking Oswald in his distress.

"Help! Someone!" he wails in desperation, finally drawing his sword. "Murder! Murder!" he cries feebly and is about to swing his weapon at Kent when, to his amazement, Edmund arrives with a detachment of armed guards to break up the fight.

"Put up your swords!" he shouts. "Stop your brawling!"

Oswald drops his sword immediately, breathing a sigh of relief.

But for Kent, clashing with the guards, the fight is just beginning. "You too, young whelp!" he fumes defiantly, battling his way through the guards until he stands before Edmund. "Come on, young master!" Moving fast, the guards charge up behind him, only to find themselves under attack by the King's men who have drawn their swords and are coming to Kent's aid, none of them aware that soldiers directed by the Duke of Cornwall are streaming into the castle yard.

While her husband charges into the fray, Regan keeps Gloucester well back of the melee. "Why weapons? Why fighting?" he asks, distraught. "What is going on?"

Cornwall has moved rapidly forward to relieve Edmund, who with his wounded arm is no match for Kent. "Quiet if you value your lives!" he shouts, a commanding presence. "He *dies* who makes the next move!" In moments the fighting subsides and silence falls over the moonlit yard, Cornwall glaring coldly at Kent, Oswald and the King's men. "Now, what is this about?" he demands to know.

"These are the messengers from our sister and the King," Regan informs him.

"What is the cause of your quarrel?" Cornwall casts a reproving look at Kent then Oswald. "Speak."

"I'm quite out of breath," Oswald pants as he brushes himself off and fusses to straighten out his clothes.

"Little wonder," Kent sneers, "when your bravery is put to such a test and so miserably fails. You're not a man," he says in disdain " – a tailor made you."

"You are an unusual fellow," says Cornwall, frowning, "a tailor make a man?"

"A tailor, sir. A sculptor or a painter wouldn't have botched the job so badly, even if they were blind and hopeless at their trade."

"What do you say?" Cornwall turns to Oswald. "What began this quarrel?"

Oswald eyes the guards who are restraining Kent. "This elderly ruffian, sir, whose life I was good enough to spare on account of his gray beard – "

Livid, Kent springs at Oswald so forcefully it's all the guards can do to hold him. "My lord," he appeals to Cornwall, "with your permission I'll pound this lump of dung into a paste and plaster it on the privy walls where it belongs." He turns on Oswald. "Spared me because of my gray beard? That will be the day – " He reacts with surprising strength and lunges at Oswald, dragging three guards with him.

"Peace, sir!" Cornwall snaps and touches the point of his sword to Kent's throat. "You unruly knave, have you no respect?"

"I do sir, but my anger is justified."

"Justified or not, what is it that makes you so angry?" Cornwall lowers his sword and peers curiously at Kent.

"That such a poor excuse for a man should be wearing a sword when he knows naught how to use it, nor even how a decent man should act. It's smiling rats like him who turn families, friends and honest people against each other, catering to every whim or impulse their lords may have, with right and wrong of no concern provided their masters are pleased and get their way. They blow with the wind these super-serviceable dogs, having no direction of their own but an eagerness to do whatever they are told, so long as it offers the promise of some reward." Oswald's response is a haughty grin that sets Kent off again.

"Curse your mocking smile, you weasel! If I had you away from here I'd wipe the laughter from your face and send you back where you came from, never to curl your lickspittle lips again!"

The vehemence of his answer makes Cornwall wince. "Have you lost your mind, fellow?"

"How did you come to be fighting, tell us that," asks Gloucester.

"No two adversaries hold more enmity toward one another than this rodent and I."

"Why would you call him that? What has he done that you should dislike him so?"

"The sight of him offends me."

"Perhaps the sight of me does too," Cornwall suggests. Or of him," he looks to Gloucester, "or her," he glances at Regan.

"Sir, I am in the habit of saying what is on my mind: I have glimpsed many better faces in my time than any I see before me at this moment."

Cornwall meets Kent's eyes with an indignant stare before looking to Regan and Gloucester. "Having at some point been praised for his bluntness, this fellow seems to have taken upon himself a contrary impudence whereby he puts the truth to use, but not for its proper purpose. Flattery, or so he would have us believe, is beyond him. With a conscience which, again, he leads us to think is honest to a fault, he puts forward his so-called truth, apparently careless as to how it's received. If people accept it, that is fine. Yet if they don't, he is compelled to let them know exactly his opinion of them. I know his type: beneath their crafty guise of bluntness they conceal their real intentions, which are more devious and divisive than the motives of twenty bowing and scraping servants ever could be."

"Sir, in good faith and utmost truthfulness," Kent comes back, "if you would permit me here in your august and illuminating presence, whose illustrious light shines on high like the radiance of the sun's flaming countenance – "

"What are you trying to say?" Cornwall demands.

Kent shrugs calmly. "Only that I will change my manner of speaking since you dislike it so. You see, sir, I can't help it that I am not a flattering man. He that used plain speaking to persuade you I was, could not have been speaking plainly, since this is not what I wish to be taken for, sir – a plain speaker that is – when I know it would only displease you more for me to speak as though I were."

His patience exhausted, Cornwall turns on Oswald. "What was it you did that this man should take such offence?"

"Nothing at all," Oswald protests innocently. "Recently it pleased the King to strike me when he misunderstood something I had said to him, whereupon this man put himself in league with the King his master, encouraged him to think I had been less than respectful, and proceeded to trip me viciously from behind. Being down, he insulted me then heaped all manner of ranting abuse upon me so his malicious efforts were taken as bravery, which drew effusive praise from the King, although from the outset I had deliberately chosen not to fight back. Having found himself thus commended on this previous occasion, when he saw me here tonight he drew his sword and made a more ruthless attack on me than before."

Cornwall glances at Kent accusingly.

Kent shrugs. "It seems I am outdone by cowards and blustering idiots," he offers placidly.

"Fetch forth the stocks!" Cornwall explodes. "You proud, stubborn old man: this will teach you!"

"Sir, I am too old to learn," Kent replies. "Don't waste your stocks on one like me. Besides, I serve the King, on whose business I was sent to you. You will show grave disrespect and unseemly malice against the grace and dignity of my sovereign master by placing his messenger in the stocks."

"Bring the stocks!" Cornwall calls again. "He shall sit there till noon tomorrow."

"Till noon?" Regan questions as she comes to stand at her husband's side. "Till night, my lord," she says with a close-lipped smile, "and another night too."

"Why, madam, if I were your father's dog you would not treat me so."

"Sir, being his servant, I will treat you as I please."

"This is the same fellow whose insolence we were warned about by our sister," Cornwall remarks as his men prepare the wooden stocks.

"Let me beseech your grace not to do this," pleads Gloucester. "His fault is serious yet the good King his master will take him to account for it, and rebuke him soundly, I am sure. This manner of punishment is one to which low wretches are condemned for common offences. The King will take it ill that his valued messenger should be treated in such a way."

"I'll answer for it," Cornwall replies.

"My sister," Regan adds pointedly, "could take it even worse to know her gentleman was abused and assaulted while tending to *her* affairs." She watches the soldiers sit Kent in the stocks and lock them together with his head and arms through the holes. "Put in his legs," she orders. The soldiers lift his ankles and fasten them into the bottom holes of the stocks, Kent not bothering to look up while they do so.

Cornwall turns and starts for the castle, Regan joining him. "Come, my lord, let us go in..."

But Gloucester remains behind until only he and Kent are left in the moonlit castle yard. "I am sorry for you, friend, 'tis the Duke's disposition which the world well knows will not be changed or stopped, once he has made up his mind. However, I will speak to him about this directly."

"No sir, please do not. I have traveled hard and not rested all the while. I'll pass some time sleeping, the rest I'll whistle." He notices Gloucester's distress. "A good man has his own share of troubles to bear." Gloucester smiles weakly. "Go in, sir. Good night till tomorrow."

"The Duke's to blame for this!" Gloucester blusters. "It will not be well received." He stews a moment longer then hurries across the yard toward a door where servants are waiting with torches to light his way inside.

Alone now, Kent forces his arm as far through the stock hole as he can and reaches below, his fingers plucking a letter from the pocket inside his jacket. Using only the one hand, he carefully unfolds it and holds it up to the light.

"Shine down, beacon of the night," he says in a prayerful voice, "so that by your cheery beams I may peruse this letter." He reads for a moment. "It is from Cordelia," he says, looking up hopefully, "who most fortunately has been told of my changed appearance. '...*and shall find time and occasion,*' " he reads again, "'*being at a safe remove from the danger there, to right these wrongs with which the realm is now beset.*'" He reads a moment more but is seized by a yawn. "Worn I know you are and craving sleep, so close yourselves heavy eyes...no need to longer view my shameful plight. Fortune, good night: smile upon your faithful servant so that he may rise and look upon the world again tomorrow..." His eyes closing, he rests his chin on the lip of the hole he has his head through, and drifts off to sleep....

Dawn's orange-pink light is flaring in the east as Edgar makes his way stealthily along the wooded road, glancing behind and in front as he goes to make sure the way is clear. Still wearing the clothes he had on when he fled his father's castle, he slows approaching a bridge, then stops when he hears something: the sound of horses coming fast on the other side.

He gets off the road quickly and enters the woods, moving among the trees with difficulty since the underbrush is thick and tangled. Soon he stops to catch his breath and looks back to the road: a dozen horsemen have crossed the bridge and stopped, several pointing with their swords at the woods.

On the run again, he glances at the trees, which are all too high for climbing and bare besides, having shed their scarlet and yellow autumn burden. He steps up his pace but has only taken a few faster strides when he trips on something underfoot and tumbles to the forest floor. Looking up from the ground, he gazes at the bearded head of a man rising from under the leaves in which he's been buried. He gawks at Edgar with a blank stare and offers a pleased, toothless grin. "Turlygod," he says simply, and gets to his feet.

Edgar has twisted his ankle in the fall. He picks himself up and tries to walk but it's too painful. He slumps to the ground, watching as the man approaches him, his bone-thin beggar's body covered in filth, naked except for a ragged piece of cloth around his loins, his wild mane of brown hair matted with thorns, prickles and burrs…

A shout goes up on the road. The man, looking to Edgar, sees his fear of the horses that are suddenly crashing through the trees toward them, and reaches for his hand. Working quickly, he brings Edgar to the place where he lay buried. He points Edgar to lie down and rapidly scoops leaves by the armful to cover him up, finishing only a moment before the horsemen charge into the clearing and surround him.

"Edgar of Gloucester is wanted," a soldier barks, eyeing the man suspiciously.

"The ports are all watched," another adds gruffly, "there is no place where guards and vigilant folk aren't looking to arrest this man."

The man walks up to a soldier with his hands cupped in front of him. "Turlygod?" The soldier only glares down, so the man moves to the next horse and holds up his hands to the soldier in the saddle. "Turlygod?"

Several soldiers climb down from their horses, draw their swords and search the area beyond the clearing. The man scampers behind them and holds out his hands in expectation. "Turlygod?"

The soldier who spoke first takes a last, quick look around before ordering the others to mount up, and soon they're headed back to the road, the man staring silently after them until they are gone. He scurries over and kneels down where he buried Edgar, clearing leaves away from his face. "Turlygod," he says and points to himself, helping Edgar to sit up.

Edgar stares into the man's crazed eyes. "Turlygod," he repeats.

"*Poor* Turlygod," the man corrects him, then points at Edgar sitting in the leaves across from him: "Poor *Tom!*"

Light from the early morning sun steals across the grounds of Gloucester's castle yard, which is deserted except for Kent, who is sleeping: his arms, head and legs still fastened in the stocks. The great wooden gates at the entrance to the yard stand open, but strangely, no one is about for the arrival of King Lear and a handful of his knights. They walk their horses further into the yard before dismounting, one of Lear's men coming forward to help the Fool from his place in the saddle behind the King.

"'Tis strange they should have left to come here and not sent back my messenger," Lear remarks.

"From what I was told," his knight says, "their departure had not been expected."

Hearing their voices, Kent awakens in the stocks and looks over. "Hail to thee, noble master."

Down from his horse, Lear turns. "Ha," he laughs out loud, "this is some strange way of enjoyment."

"It is not that, my lord," Kent says, ashamed.

"My, my," the Fool chimes in, "'tis indeed as strange a pair of stockings as I've ever seen a man wear." He chuckles. "Horses are tethered around the head, dogs and bears by the neck, monkeys around the middle, but men…by their *legs*? Though perhaps a man with a weakness for wandering could be kept in place wearing such things," he says with a shrug.

"Who is he that would so much mistake your place as to put you here like this?" Lear asks, walking over.

"It is both he and she, your son and daughter."

"No."

"Yes."

"No, I say."

"I say yes."

"No, no, they would not."

"Yes yes, they would."

"By Jupiter, I swear no."

"By his wife I swear yes."

"They *wouldn't* – 'tis worse than murder doing something so outrageous to a messenger of the King. What could prompt them to think you deserving of this treatment, when knowing you had come from us?"

"My lord," Kent answers, "reaching their castle I duly delivered Your Highness's letters to them. Before I had even got up from my bowing, there came a desperate messenger, out-of-breath, his clothes soaked through in sweat, who with much gasping and panting presented salutations which were from his mistress, Goneril. He delivered letters at the same time, in spite of his having interrupted me, which they promptly read and, on the strength of whose contents they summoned their people and ordered them to make ready for travel here, to my Duke of Gloucester. Mounting their horses straightaway, they commanded me to follow if I would, and said, with cool and surly looks, that they would afford me an answer when it happened they could. Arriving here, whom did I meet but the other messenger, whose welcome by your daughter Regan had far exceeded that provided me – this the selfsame fellow who lately showed his rude disrespect towards Your Majesty. Anger bettering my wisdom, I drew my sword on the villain and cursed him. His frightened cries raised such a loud and cowardly alarm that your son and daughter deemed my having drawn and spoken out against him, to merit the shame which here I suffer."

"The trouble's far from done: it's only just begun!" the Fool pipes up mischievously. "'*Fathers that wear rags,*'" he begins a droll ditty, "'*their children have nothing for sharing. But fathers that bear moneybags,*" *their children are filled with caring. Fortune, the stingy whore, has never a hand out to the poor!'"* he scolds, producing an apple from under his coat which he puts in one of Kent's hands, while into the other he slips a crust of bread…

"O, how dread the feeling that wells up within my heart once more," Lear says dolefully, struggling to keep his composure. "Hold off, consuming anger, plague me not mounting sorrow – your place is not here, not now." He puts a badly shaking hand to his forehead and rubs his brow. A moment later he turns to Kent. "Where is this daughter?" he demands.

"Inside, sir, with her husband."

Lear starts for the castle, the Fool and the knight following right behind until he stops and waves them off. "Don't come with me. Stay here for now." He continues on across the yard and approaches a door upon which he bangs with the handle of his horsewhip when it won't open…

"Is there something else than what you've said?" the Fool asks Kent. "You did no more than draw your sword, and curse?"

"Nothing," Kent says, noticing the handful of knights waiting beside their horses. "How is it that the King comes with so few of his men?"

"If you were put in the stocks for a question like that," the Fool comes back, " then surely you deserved it."

"But why is it, Fool?" Kent persists.

The Fool saunters back to the stocks. "All that followed him are not blind," he says, studying the padlock on the hinge holding the upper planks closed around Kent's head and arms, "and if they were, there's not a nose among them but can sniff the scent of trouble. You see, sir, when the great wheel begins to roll down hill, that's the time to let go, lest you break your neck with hanging on. Thus too, when the next great one goes upward, you cling tightly so it pulls you up behind. When a wise man offers better advice than this, be so good as to give me mine back again." He considers several pins he has brought out from under his jester's cap. "Of course," he continues, inserting the middle-sized pin in the keyhole of the padlock, "I would only want fools to follow this, sir, since a Fool gives it. *'The man who serves others hoping to gain,*" he recites as he works on picking the lock, "*but does it just in show, will pack and fly when it starts to rain, and storm winds blow and blow.*'" He puts his ear to the padlock and listens. "But I will tarry," he affirms matter-of-factly. "The Fool will stay, and let the wise man go. The fool is foolish who runs away." He pauses. "This Fool?" He gives the pin a precise, careful twist and the iron padlock clicks open. " – No fool, I say."

"Where learned you this Fool?" Kent grins.

"Not in the stocks," the Fool winks and is kneeling to start on the lower lock when a door to the castle flies open and Lear storms into the yard.

"Will not *speak* with me?" he fumes at Gloucester, who hurries out a moment later and follows close behind. "They're *sick*," he says with a mocking sneer, "they're *tired* from traveling in the night. These are but cunning excuses!" he erupts, "the seeds of dissension, the guise of revolt! Fetch me a better answer!"

"My dear lord," Gloucester fumbles, "you know the Duke's fiery temperament, how firm and immovable he is when once he has made up his mind – "

"Sickness and vengeance," Lear fires back. "Death and destruction!" He takes a few more steps then stops and turns to Gloucester. "Fiery? Temperament?" he questions pointedly. "I wish to speak with the Duke of Cornwall and his wife!" he rails as he continues toward the stocks.

"Of course, my good lord, I informed them of that."

"In*form*ed them? Do you not understand me, man?"

"I do, my good lord."

Lear wheels again, grabbing Gloucester roughly by the shirt and pulling him close. "The King would like to speak with Cornwall," he says coldly, "the dear father would like to speak with his daughter, commands – desires – expects to be obeyed! Inform them of *that*!" he explodes and lets go of Gloucester. "By my breath and blood, *fiery*? The *fiery* Duke?" He throws Gloucester an infuriated frown. "Tell the *hot* Duke that Lear – no, not yet – "

Strangely, he breaks off and looks away, the bells on the Fool's cap jingling just below as he puts an ear to the lower padlock and listens. "It may be that he *isn't* well," Lear acknowledges. "Sickness can cause us to neglect those formalities which good health observes. We are not quite ourselves when illness takes over, forcing the mind to suffer along with the body…" He glances at Gloucester, who is keeping his distance, even though Lear's tantrum appears to have subsided. "I'll let it pass, impatience having provoked me to mistake a man who is not well, for one who is." Gloucester nods, relieved, but then Lear notices Kent and his anger is touched off again. "Why in the name of *majesty* is this man still sitting here?" he demands. "Why, an act such as this – I can't but be persuaded there is something to the Duke and her avoiding me. – Set my man free!" he hollers at Gloucester. "Go you and tell the Duke and his wife I wish to speak with them, now, without delay: bid them come out and hear me or I'll beat on their chamber door till sleepless they beg me to stop."

"I hope all can be well between you," Gloucester offers as he quickly bows and goes.

Lear hunches his shoulders and presses a fist against his chest. "O my heart," he winces in obvious pain, "my swelling heart. Stop I say!"

"You cry like the innocent maid," the Fool teases, "when her first love proved too eager. 'Stop, I say, stop!' she cried, for the swelling was not in his heart…" The lower padlock picked, he begins to remove it, but Kent catches his eye and motions with his head toward the castle: Cornwall, Regan and Gloucester, followed by a full entourage of soldiers, servants and attendants, are making their way over to speak with Lear.

"Good morrow to you both," he says cordially when they present themselves.

"Hail to your grace," Cornwall bows respectfully.

"I am glad to see Your Highness," Regan says.

"I think you are," Lear replies, "and I know why I should think so. If you were not, I would say the woman in your mother's tomb had been unfaithful to me."

Regan lets the remark pass, her attention on Kent who is out of the stocks and being helped to his feet by the Fool. The sun has gone in and a stiffening breeze begun to blow through the castle yard.

"So you are free," Lear remarks as Kent takes a place beside him.

"Well…some other time for that. – Beloved Regan," he carries on, "your sister is wicked. She has set the vulture unkindness to feed on me here." He puts a hand to his heart. "I can barely speak of it," he says, his voice filled with resentment, "you'll not believe how depraved she has been toward me – O, Regan!" Choking back tears, he turns away, trembling…

"Take courage, sir, I pray you: I'm sure it was only that you failed to see all she was doing for you, not she who failed in what she saw as her duty to you."

He gives her a wary look. "What mean you by that?"

"I can't believe but that my sister would live up to her every obligation. If, sir, she happened to impose restraint on your riotous followers, it would only have been with much good reason and prudent purpose – she should not be blamed."

"My curses on her."

"Good sir, you are old. Your life approaches the limit of its course: you need tending and caring for by someone who knows the state of things better than you yourself. Therefore I suggest you return to our sister and acknowledge you have wronged her."

"Ask her forgiveness? Can you not see how unbecoming that would be to me, a king and father?" He kneels down. "Dear daughter," he pleads, "I admit that I am old, that no one has need for those of my age. On my knees I beg that you might grant me food and clothing, and let me live henceforth with you."

"Enough," she says sharply. "These tricks do not become you. Do what is required and return to my sister, sir."

"Never, Regan," he declares and gets to his feet. "She has stripped me of half my train, upbraided and disdained me – stung me with her poison tongue and hurt me to the quick. Let all the wrath of heaven fall hard and cruel upon her: cripple her bones with lameness and leave her for – "

"No sir, no," Cornwall insistently cautions.

But there is no stopping the King. " – Lightning sear her scornful eyes to blindness," he rants, "her beauty blister into sores the sun will scorch until they bleed – "

"By the gods," Regan objects, "you will wish the same on me

when a cross mood strikes!"

"No, Regan," he protests and quickly regains his composure. "You shall never have my curse: your tenderhearted nature is not given to scorn like hers. Her eyes are cold and spiteful, where yours are warm and kind. 'Tis not in you to thwart my pleasures nor my pastimes, to deprive me of my knights, sling sharp words, deplete my stipend or worst than all else, bar the very door against your father. You better know the bonds of childhood, the tokens of courtesy, the proper shows of gratitude." He fixes her with a stare. "And also, you will not have forgotten the half of this my kingdom with which you were endowed."

"To the point, good sir," Regan says and meets her father's eyes but only briefly: horns signal an arriving party beyond the castle gate.

"Whose trumpets are these?" Cornwall asks uneasily.

"*Who* put my man in the stocks?" Lear returns to his demand.

"They are my sister's," Regan answers Cornwall. "She wrote that she would be here." She notices Oswald emerging from the castle. He runs swiftly over to stand with her. "This is your lady is it not?" she asks him.

Spotting Oswald, Lear snarls in derision, " – This is a slave, whose merit is no more than pleasing the fickle graces of the mistress he follows. Out of my sight, you dog!" He moves to strike Oswald but Cornwall intervenes.

" – What means this, Your Grace?"

"Who *stocked* my servant?" Lear resumes angrily, "Regan, I am hopeful you knew nothing of this."

Ignoring him, she gazes at the castle gate where Goneril is riding in, her soldiers deploying quickly on both sides of the castle yard as Goneril brings her horse to a halt and gets down, without help from the grooms who have rushed to assist her.

Brushing back her hair, which the strengthening wind is blowing against her face, Regan leaves her father and walks over to bid Goneril welcome. Lear grows more perturbed as his eyes take in the soldiers on their horses, armed.

"O heaven above, what is this…" he murmurs to himself. "If you care for old men may your guiding power hold sway. If you yourselves are old, make my cause your own. O Gods, send down and take my – " He breaks off, bewildered, as Goneril and Regan greet each other. "Are you not ashamed, Regan, to look upon her face?" he calls. "And you take her by the hand as well?"

"Why not by the hand, sir?" Goneril comes back. "How can I have wronged you? Things are not offences because bad judgment and your dotage deem them so."

"O heart, may you keep from bursting," Lear tries to contain himself, but cannot. "How came my man to be in the *stocks*?" he explodes yet again.

"I set him there, sir," Cornwall admits, "though his conduct deserved much worse."

"You?" Lear winces, confused.

Regan comes up and takes his arm. "I pray you, father, being weak now, it is best that you behave so. If you will return to my sister and stay this month with her, dismissing half your train of knights, you are welcome to come to me. I am presently away from home and so am not provisioned as is needful for your proper custom."

"Return to her? With fifty knights dismissed? No," he declares firmly, "I'd rather live in the wild and fend for myself alone against the elements – be comrades with the wolf and the owl, suffer the bitterest hardships if I must. Return to her? Why, the hot-blooded France who took our youngest-born without dowry, I could just as well kneel at his feet and beg a paltry pension out of pity. Return with her? I'd bow and scrape for this detested lackey," he shifts his eyes at Oswald, "before I'd ever darken her door again."

"The choice is yours, sir," Goneril tells him, undaunted.

Lear meets her eyes with a threatening glare. "I pray you, daughter," he warns, "do not make me mad." Goneril only gazes at him. "I will not trouble you further, my child. Farewell." He motions to Kent and the Fool that he is leaving, but doesn't move. "We'll not meet again, you and I. No more see one another. For though you are my flesh and blood – my daughter – you are a disease infecting my flesh that now has become my own. You are a boil, a festering sore: a pus-oozing ulcer in my sickened blood! But let me not reproach you." Goneril smirks at this. "No, let shame come to you when it will. I invoke it not, I do not bid Jupiter condemn you nor do I disparage you before Juno who judges from on high. Heal yourself at such time as you are able to, get better at your leisure. I can be patient, I can stay with Regan, my hundred knights and I," he says with a gloating smile.

"Not entirely, sir," Regan corrects him. "As was said, I am not expecting you until a month from now, and again as I did say, am presently unable to offer you a fit welcome. Listen to my sister, sir," she pleads. "For as with her, any who in the light of reason consider how you have conducted yourself of late, will see and understand that it is only because you are old, and so – but I should not speak for her…"

"Is this truly spoken, Regan?" he asks, bewildered.

"Truly spoken, sir," she answers quickly. "But fifty followers! That is still a goodly train. What need would you have of more – indeed, or even that many – since both expense and trouble argue against retaining so great a number? Besides, it will be hard, if not impossible, for so many to get along under one roof while taking orders from different masters."

"Wouldn't you be as well attended by her servants and mine?" Goneril suggests.

"Why not, my lord?" Regan asks, moving to stand with Goneril. "If then they were to slacken in their duties, my sister and I could look to it ourselves." She considers for a moment. "On better thought, if you desire to come and stay with me I entreat you to bring but five and twenty: to no more than this would I give accommodation."

"I gave you all – " Lear reminds her sternly.

"And it was right you did so," Regan acknowledges.

" – I made you the guardians and protectors of my power, but kept the right to be followed by a certain number. You would have me come with five and twenty?" he looks to Regan. "Is that what you said?"

"And will again, my lord: no more than that with me."

Lear turns away in contemplation. "Hideous creatures seem pleasing when others more hideous present themselves," he reasons. "Not being the worst between two is something… " He looks to Goneril. "I'll go with thee. Thy fifty is double her twenty-five, yours twice the love of hers."

"Hear me, my lord," says Goneril. "What need have you for five and twenty? For ten? Or five? To attend you in a house where twice that number will be called upon to serve you?"

"What need for one?" asks Regan.

"Reason not the *need*!" Lear shouts, his temper bursting. "Even the basest beggars have trifles they do not *need*. Allow a man no more than what he *needs* to stay alive, and his life is cheap as a beast's. You are a lady," he looks Regan up and down, "if warmth were in the wearing of fine clothes you'd have no need for these you're dressed in now, whose least purpose is to keep you warm. But for true need – O you heavens: give me that patience – patience I need! You see me here you gods, a poor old man, as full of grief as age, wretched in both: if it is you that stirs these daughters' hearts against their father, don't make me such a fool to bear it tamely. Touch me with noble anger. Never let unmanly tears be seen upon this face. No, you unnatural hags, I will wreak such havoc and revenge upon you both, that all the world shall – I will do *such* things – what they are I know not yet, but they shall be the horrors of the earth! You think I'll weep?" The question hangs in the air momentarily. "No," he says bitterly, "I'll not weep." With that he turns and starts toward the gate, the Fool walking beside him, while Kent, whose legs are stiff from his night in the stocks, limps slowly along behind, helped by the Duke of Gloucester who is in despair over what is happening.

"I have perfect cause for weeping!" Lear shouts for all to hear. "But this heart would have to break into a hundred thousand pieces before I'd ever weep! O Fool," he says as he reaches the gate and passes through, "I shall go mad…"

Cornwall motions for several servants to take the stocks away then glances up at the darkening sky, the flags atop Gloucester's castle flapping in the steadily gusting wind. "The storm is nearing," he warns, "we best go in."

"What of the old man?" Regan asks and walks with him.

"'Tis no fault of ours," he tells her and makes way for Goneril to join them. "He has done this to himself and must taste the fruits of his own foolishness."

"Himself I would gladly receive," Regan explains, "but not one of his followers."

"I am of the same mind," Goneril agrees, raising her voice to be heard over the sound of the driving wind. Thunder cracks overhead and the first drops of rain begin to fall. She looks to Cornwall. "Where is my lord of Gloucester?"

"Followed the old man forth," he says, unconcerned.

"The King – " a voice calls out behind them.

Regan turns to see Gloucester struggling hard against the wind as he makes his way through the castle yard. "He is returning," she says to Cornwall.

The rain pouring in earnest now, Gloucester reaches the others and halts to catch his breath. "The King," he pants, "is in high rage."

"Where is he going?" Cornwall asks and helps Gloucester toward the castle door.

"He calls for his horse but I know not where he is bound."

"To let him have his way would be best," Cornwall advises. "His is not a frame of mind that will be reasoned with."

"Therefore you must use all means to keep him away," Goneril warns.

"But the winds are fierce," he protests, "for miles around there's scarcely a tree and little shelter to be found."

"Good sir," Regan explains, shouting above the driving rain, "the harm he brings upon himself is the only thing a stubborn man will learn from. Close your doors to him, my good lord. His followers are desperate men, and in his present state there is no telling what they could incite him to."

Gloucester nods gravely, but when the others have gone inside he remains behind, looking gloomily out from the doorway into the worsening storm....

It is night and the storm raging over the countryside near Gloucester's castle shows no signs of letting up as Kent makes his way through a barren field against the wind and driving rain. Thunder bursting in the darkness overhead, his face is illuminated with each flash of lightning, washed clean now of the char smudge he used to disguise his appearance. Limping badly, he winces as he walks on, but soon is in too much pain to continue. He collapses on the sodden ground, rain pouring hard on his bowed head and shivering shoulders while he rubs the calves of his legs.

Before long he gets back on his feet, cupping his hands over his eyes while he decides in which direction to go. Starting out, he hasn't gone far when up ahead he notices an armed soldier who has got down from the saddle to lead his frightened horse by the reins, the desperate animal whinnying in fear, reluctant to go forward.

"Who's there, besides foul weather?" Kent calls over.

"One minded like the weather, sir!" the man yells back. In a few moments he reaches Kent, his tall boots splashing through puddles on the ground, his shoulders hunched together against the punishing deluge. His hair is slicked down against the sides of his face and his clothes have long been drenched through: water running off the tip of his nose, he looks half drowned. He steadies his horse, gives a dismal shake of his head. "All the day and now into the night," he says, disquieted, but breaks off when lightning flashes just above them and a crack of thunder explodes a moment later, the horse rearing up on its hind legs in alarm.

Recognizing him as one of the knights who was with the King at
Gloucester's castle, Kent peers closely when the man regains control
of his animal. "I know you, sir," he says.

Squinting through the rain, the man looks at Kent uncertainly and
shrugs.

"Where's the King?" Kent asks him.

"Contending with the frightful elements," the knight answers.
"Commands the wind to blow the earth into the sea, or have its
cresting waves surge overland and ruin all, or cease its fury altogether,
tears out his white hair, which the whipping wind scatters like meager
bits of fluff, strives in his little human way to overrule the storm itself
in the violence of his desperate, shouting rage. And on a night when
bears, nor lions nor wolves upon the brink of their starvation would
dare venture forth, he runs upon the hillside with neither hat nor coat,
defying the forces above to take all from him, or nothing."

"But who is with him?"

"Only his Fool, who tries with jesting to lighten the King's pain-
afflicted heart."

"Sir, I know you," Kent insists, "and on the strength of what you
say entrust you with some knowledge that most concerns our king.
Although it is yet secret and far from common knowledge, there is
bitter and devious striving among the dukes of Albany and Cornwall.
And as is bound to happen with those whose stars are on the rise and
great destiny within their grasp, spies in the service of France are
placed within the dukes' respective camps, circulating word as to the
state of things between their rival masters, their movements and
maneuvering for power, their cruelty to the old and well loved king –
and things more deeply hidden in addition, to which these measures
give dangerous indication. As well, it is confirmed from France there
comes a force who in our coastal ports have gained a foothold, and are
almost at the point of making known the cause they fight for, is the
saving of our King. Now to you: if, crediting the news I have
unfolded, you speed for Dover, you shall find those who will with
grateful ears, receive what you can tell them of our current state, chief
of all, the deep and maddening sorrow the King has been made to
suffer, in which he has good cause to feel betrayed. I am a gentleman

of blood and noble breeding, who in loyalty to the King do ask you this favor."

"We shall talk further of this!" the knight replies after a booming clap of thunder.

"No, we cannot!" Kent comes back quickly. He undoes his belt and removes a small pouch. "To prove I am much more than my poor clothes would have you believe, open this and see what it contains." Unfastening the pouch, he reaches in and takes out the gold medallion chain that he wore as advisor to the King. "If you see Cordelia, as I have no doubt you shall, show her that, and she will tell you who this fellow is that yet you do not know."

The knight's horse rears, hooves kicking in the air close to his head. "A curse upon this storm!" he cries. "Give me your hand!" Kent hurries putting out his hand, and they shake. "Is there anything more to know?" the knight asks.

"Nothing that cannot wait until we've found the King. You go in that direction," he points ahead, "I'll go in this," he cocks his thumb behind, holding the knight's horse while he mounts up. "Who comes upon him first, alert the other..."

They head their separate directions, quickly disappearing into the blinding rain....

The storm reaching the height of its fury, thunder booms like cannon fire in concert with the lightning, Lear stalking back and forth high on the top of a hill as he shouts at the sky in vehement rage, fists raised, his shirt torn open, his wet, white hair lying flat against his skull, while his Fool sits haplessly on the ground nearby, shoes off, wringing out his socks, water streaming around his legs and off the bells on the sagging tips of his fool's cap.

"Blow winds and crack your cheeks!" Lear rails in frenzied anger, though more of his words are drowned in the drumming rain and exploding thunder than can be heard. "Rage, blow – you cataracts and hurricanoes spout, till you have drenched our steeples, drowned our rooves – you sulphurous and thought-executing fires, hot couriers of oak-cleaving thunderbolts, singe my white head! And thus, all-shaking thunder strike flat the thick rotundity of the world, crack nature's moulds, let human seed spew forth no more that makes ungrateful man – "

"Nuncle," the Fool pipes up, "your flattering speeches are better given in a dry house than out here in the pelting rain! Go in, good Nuncle," he gibes, "and ask your daughters' blessing: this is a night that pities neither wise men nor fools."

" – Rumble thy belly full!" Lear resumes his shouting. "Spit fire, spout rain – nor you, nor wind, nor fire are my daughters! I fault you not, you elements, for unkindness – I never gave *you* a kingdom, called you my children. You owe me no allegiance – let fall your worst upon me: I stand here a slave to your will, a poor, infirm, weak and despised old man. Though why you should enlist my two pernicious daughters in your heavenly battalion to assail a head so old and white as mine, is too foul, 'tis foul…" Weary and despairing, he hobbles over and sits down with the Fool, staring blindly out at the steadily pouring rain.

"He that has a house to keep his head in, has a good head, sir," the Fool quips pointedly then gets to his feet when he notices Lear is shivering. He searches around until he finds Lear's cloak. "A man who takes a woman to house before his heart is ready," he says, bringing back the cloak and draping it over the King's head, "will have no more than a poor church mouse, and troubles hard and steady." He kneels down, has Lear lift a foot and starts removing his boots. "But the man who puts his trust and faith, in what his jealous daughters sayeth – and banishes the one who will not speak, has no one but himself to blame for being old and weak. For never was a woman fair, but practiced faces in her mirror." He watches as Lear peers out from under his cloak and down at his bare feet, wiggling his toes slightly as the rainwater rushes over them…

"No," he murmurs tiredly, and looks up. "I will be the model of patience. I will say nothing…"

The Fool shrugs and is moving to sit down again when he catches sight of someone clambering up the hill toward them.

"Who's there?" a voice calls through the rain.

"One with a crown and one without," the Fool answers cheekily, "that is to say a wise man and a fool..." He stands in front of the King and, in the still flickering lightning, soon makes out a familiar limping figure.

"What, sir," Kent says hurrying forward, "what do you up *here*? Even that which loves the night loves not a night like this," he scolds, crouching in front of the King and taking stock: he finds the King's boots and begins putting them back on. "The wrathful skies do frighten even the creatures of the dark so they stay hidden in their caves on a night like this…In all my years I've never seen such flashing in the sky nor felt such tremors of bursting thunder. Such wails of roaring wind and rain – the best of men can hardly bear such torment and such fear without affliction." He stands up and waits for Lear to rise, but he only stares blankly forward and doesn't move. Kent turns to the Fool and waves him to help: together they bend down to lift the King, but Lear pushes their hands away.

"Let the great gods that keep such turmoil overhead know sinners by the fear there's no disguising, he says, his voice somber. Tremble, you that have within you crimes you've not confessed, things you've not been punished for. Hide, you with blood on your hands, you who have perjured yourselves, and you, incestuous pretenders who will smile in seeming virtue. Shake, wretch, to your very bones, in fear of secrets and hypocrisy that plot against a man and bring him down. Release what's been concealed inside too long. Your grievous guilts divulge. Trust…unto the mercy of those who summon you to be judged, who need hear this: I am a man more sinned against than sinning."

"My gracious lord," Kent says with urgency, "not far from here is a hovel: some shelter it will lend you from the storm." He and the Fool help Lear onto his feet. "Rest you there and I to this cold castle will return – cold, because in asking after you just now, they firmly did deny me to come in. I'll force them to make up that stinted courtesy to me, and have them know you must be taken in – "

"My wits begin to turn," Lear says, takes off the boots that Kent has just put on, and gets to his feet. He looks to the Fool, who is shivering badly. "Are you cold, my boy? "I am cold myself," he says, and turns to Kent. "Where is this hovel you speak of fellow?" Kent points the way and starts walking. "The art of our necessities is strange," Lear says to his companions as they go, "when the worst of things can be made precious. Poor fool and knave, a piece of my heart is sorry for the trouble I've caused thee."

"*He that has just a little tiny wit,*" the Fool sings, "*with a hey, ho: the wind and the rain, must be content as fortune sees fit: though the rain it raineth every day.*"

"True, my good boy," says Lear and puts an arm around his shoulders.

The three figures move down hill and gradually disappear in the rain, the Fool, ever merry, jesting with the King:

"When priests deliver words that matter, brewers wet not their malt with water; when nobles become their tailors' tutors, those heretics burned but wenches' suitors; when every case in law is right, no squire in debt, nor one poor knight; when slanders have stopped being spoken with tongues, and purse-thieves decline to mingle in throngs; when lenders count their gold outdoors, and bawds and whores darken church doors – then shall the realm of Albion come to great confusion, for that is the time, who lives to see it, when going is done without the feet. This prophecy shall Merlin make, but I live before his time…."

Rain teems down on Gloucester's castle as several dozen of his soldiers, fitted with battle armor and spears, bring their horses through the darkness of the now flooded castle yard and up to the partially open gate where Gloucester stands in ankle-deep water beside his own horse, which several grooms are hurrying to make ready. Heedless of the mud that flies up from the horses' hooves as they gallop past him, he urgently waves each rider on his way until all are through then turns to check that the sack his grooms have bundled on the back of his saddle is fastened tight.

"Blankets, food and drink, my lord," a groom tells him, motioning that the chin-strap on his helmet is still undone. Gloucester fumbles with it a moment but the leather is too slippery and his hands are shaking from the cold. The groom moving to assist him, someone pulls his arm away from behind.

" – Edmund!" Gloucester jumps then sighs in relief on seeing his son, who ties the helmet strap while his father talks. "I like not this treatment of the King, Edmund. When I asked their leave to show him some mercy, they took from me the use of my own house, warned me on pain of perpetual displeasure not so much as to mention his name, nor speak to them on his behalf, nor offer him help of any kind."

"Most cruel and unbefitting," Edmund sympathizes.

"Therefore, listen carefully, but say nothing of what I tell you here. Not only is there strife between the Dukes of Cornwall and Albany, but a matter equally as serious has arisen: I did receive a letter tonight – 'tis dangerous even to speak of it – and I have locked it for protection in my chamber." He lowers his voice. "These slights and injuries the King now suffers will be revenged in kind, and soon," he explains, "as forces to relieve him are not only afoot, but marching hither from the coast. We must side with the King, Edmund – we must!" Edmund puts a cautioning finger to his lips. Gloucester nods and quiets down. "Meantime, I will search him out and offer the help I can," he points to the bundle of provisions on his horse, "which leaves you to keep conversation with Cornwall so my presence will not be missed. If he asks for me, say I am ill and gone to bed." A soldier returns to the yard, anxious over the delay. The grooms helping, Gloucester promptly mounts his horse and takes the reins. "It is no matter if I die for doing this, and they have threatened me with no less," he declares solemnly, "but my old King and master must be helped," he says with resolve. "I pray you be careful, Edmund. There is strange business stirring." He spurs his horse and goes, the castle gate closing behind him a moment later.

The grooms joining the gatekeepers to head inside, Edmund remains behind.

"This kindness that's forbidden you, shall instantly be known," he gloats, "as will your letter's news, which actions in support of him, the Duke will find deserving of reward: surely nothing less than my father's title, his lands and all. The younger rises when the old doth fall."

Smiling, he lifts his face to the falling rain and keeps it there for some time....

"Here is the place, my Lord!" Kent shouts to the King and his Fool, windblown rain beating hard on their faces as they come through the darkness and arrive at a small, thatch-roofed hut set against an ancient fieldstone fence. "Enter, my good Lord!" Kent urges the King. "The tyranny of these open skies is too much for your endurance!" A stream of water coursing off the end of his nose, he takes Lear by the arm to lead him in, but the King throws off his hand.

"Let me alone," he says.

"Good my Lord, go inside – "

"Will it break my heart?"

"I would rather it break mine own, sir," Kent comes back. "Please get you in."

"You think it matters much that this battering storm so punishes the body. And perhaps it does, but when the greater pain is borne within the mind, all other things are scarcely felt. You'd run from a bear if ever it confronted you. But if your sole escape were on the cliff above the roaring sea, you'd have to meet him face to face, as you are meeting me. When the mind is free, the body is able to feel: this tempest in my mind takes from my other senses all capacity to care, except about the single thought that beats, relentless, there: the ingratitude of children." He meets Kent's eyes for a brief moment, then turns away to peer at the surrounding darkness. "To have bitten the hand that feeds them! I will see them punished," he proclaims, "and I will stop my weeping." He glares defiantly. "But I will not weep. Shut me out, on such a night as this?" his temper flares. "Pour on!" he cries over the sound of drumming rain, "I will endure! O Regan, Goneril, on such a night as this! Your old, kind father...whose generous heart gave you all – O that way madness lies. I will shun that – no more of it…" He stares at the crude shelter: the bones of small animals strung in a row along the edge of the roof, tangled and blown by the wind…

"Good my Lord, enter here," Kent continues to plead.

"Go in yourself, sir," Lear says feelingly, "seek your own comfort. This tempest is well to keep me from pondering what could hurt me more." Kent puts his hand insistently on Lear's shoulder and brings him to the door of the hut. "I'll go in, then," Lear acquiesces. "In boy," he calls to the Fool, sitting cross-legged on the ground. "Go first, my poor wandering boy – " The Fool takes one look at the hut and promptly shakes his head, gesturing that Lear be the first to go. "But *no*," the King resists, "get *you* in, I must pray before I sleep." The Fool makes a face but reluctantly goes, Lear kneeling worshipfully before the hanging skeleton bones…

"Poor, naked wretches, wherever you may be, that suffer the pelting of this pitiless storm: how shall your bare, uncovered heads and bony sides, your torn and ragged clothes, protect you in seasons such as this? …In my life I have thought too little of these things," he reflects. "Heal thy self, Your Greatness: feel what lowly wretches feel, that henceforth you may share your plenteous bounty with them, and show the heavens more justice here – "

"Help me! Help!" the Fool cries and tears out of the hut, a voice booming inside: "Fathoms deep! Fathoms dark! Poor Tom!"

"Go not in there, Nuncle, there's a ghost!" the Fool warns and hides behind Kent.

"Give me your hand," he says and approaches the hut. "Who's there?" he demands.

"A ghost, a ghost!" the Fool insists. "He says his name's Poor Tom."

"Who are you that grumbles there?" Kent demands again. "Come forth."

A nearly naked Edgar leaps from the hut, pointing back inside. "Away, the devil chases me! Flee!" he shrieks, "flee before he catches thee, sharp winds blow in the hawthorn tree, humh?" he cries. "No! To bed and warm thee!" A crazed look on his cut and bleeding face, his hair is wild, his loins barely covered by a small, frayed cloth.

Lear gets to his feet and comes over. "Did you give all to your two daughters, and ended now like this?" He stares at Edgar's trembling body.

"Who gives anything to Poor Tom?" Edgar answers. "Whom the devil himself has led through fire and through flame," he says, speaking fast, "through stream and whirlpool, o'er quagmire and bog, placed knives beneath Tom's pillow, a noose above Tom's bed, put poison in his porridge, made him brave at heart but just to ride upon his horse across the bridge that was no more than but a lightning fallen tree, scared then by his shadow like a traitor who is hunted for. Bless your wit and fantasy, imaginings and memory, but Tom's a-cold. O *do*, dee *do*, dee *do*, dee – bless thee, and thee, and thee," he says with a look to Lear, the Fool, and Kent, "and do Poor Tom some charity, before the foul fiend – " He grabs at the air. "There – I could have caught him. And there! And there once more!" Growling and snapping with his teeth, he wrestles imaginary demons.

"Have his daughters driven him to this?" Lear puts the question. "Could you save nothing?" he asks Edgar. "Did you have to give them all?"

"No," the Fool points to the patch of cloth on his hips, "they left him at least a napkin, else we had all been ashamed."

"Now worst of harms," Lear curses, "that can a guilty man befall – descend upon your daughters all!"

"He has no daughters, sir," says Kent.

"Traitor's death! What else could bring a man to such a state as this, but unkind daughters? Is it the custom for discarded fathers to have such scant regard for their body's very flesh?" He considers the thought. "Though fitting punishment it would be – since this was the flesh that gave the monstrous daughters life."

"Pillicock lay on Pillicock's hill, alow alow, aloo aloo." Edgar makes various pantomime faces while he sings to himself: anguished, sorrowful, frightened and sad, then cups his hands and holds them out to Lear, who laughs and pretends to give him something. "This bitter night will turn us all to fools and madmen," the Fool says and rolls his eyes.

"Beware the fiend," Edgar tells him. He turns to Kent. "Obey your parents," he warns. "Take no oaths, nor break your promise neither. No adultery, sir," he wags a finger at Lear, "nor stand your sweetheart on display without her finest clothes." Lear takes him by the shoulders and peers into his eyes. "Tom's a-cold," Edgar says, his teeth chattering.

"What have you been?" Lears asks, frowning.

Edgar gawks at him. "Been?"

Lear nods. "Been."

"A lover valiant in heart and mind," Edgar answers, "my hair smoothed back, a scented rose adorning my coat, who served the lust of my mistress' heart and did the darkest deeds with her. Swore oaths as though they were any words, then broke them all in front of heaven. One I was who dreamed in sleep of lustful things and waked with lust to carry them out. Loved my wine and dice as dearly, in women my lovers numbered more than a sultan with his harem. Unfaithful I was, a flattering pandering slandering rogue who would fight for the slightest reason. Lazy as a pig, sly as a fox, greedy as a wolf, mad as a dog," he makes a snarling face, "fierce as the preying lion. Let not the shine of fashionable shoes nor the rustling of prettiest silk, entice your heart to love a woman. Yes, keep your distance from brothels, your hands from under skirts, your name from moneylenders' lists, and more than all else, defy the foul fiend at every chance." He cocks his head as though he's heard something. "Still through the trees a cold wind blows: says suum, mun, nonny. Dauphin, my boy, cessez! Let him gallop away…"

Lear stands back, his mind working. "Is man no more than this?" He looks at Edgar. "Consider him closely. You need no worm for silk," he says, "no beast for hide, no sheep for wool, no deer for the scent of perfume. You see?" He gestures to Kent and the Fool. "Here's three of us are sophisticated, but *you* are the thing itself. A man is no more than such a poor, bare, forked creature as thou art." He undoes his pants and begins tearing at his shirt. "Off, off you trappings, remove these from me – " Reacting quickly, Kent grabs his arms to restrain him. The Fool struggles to buckle up his pants.

" – Goodness, Nuncle, calm yourself," he scolds "'tis a bad night to go swimming in." Lear soon grows weak and settles down, staring dejectedly into space. "A small fire in a barren field is like an old lecher's heart," the Fool pipes up, "a spark that glows in a vast dark place: look there, a walking fire…"

A torch flame is moving toward them across the field.

"This is the foul fiend Flibbertigibbet!" Edgar cries, "he begins after dark and roams till the end of night, bringing blindness, plucking out eyes, his lisping lips spread fungus upon the ripening wheat and he preys on all the helpless creatures of the earth."

His shoulders sagging, Lear lowers his head, exhausted.

"How fares Your Grace?" Kent says and clutches him under the arms.

A voice calls out in the darkness.

"Who is that?" Lear murmurs.

"Who are you?" shouts Kent. "Whom do you seek?"

"Who are you?" the voice calls back. "Give your names!"

"Poor Tom, that eats the swimming frog," cries Edgar, "the toad, the tadpole, the lizard, the newt – that in the fury of his heart, when the foul fiend rages, eats cow dung in salads, feasts on old rats and dogs found dead in the ditch – drinks the green scum on the murky pond – who is whipped in one place after another, clamped in the stocks, punished and imprisoned – but never a suit to call his own or shirt upon his filthy back, nor a horse to ride, nor a weapon to wear, but mice and rats and some small deer, have been Tom's food for seven long year. Beware you, fiend! Peace, you devil Smulkin, peace you fiend!"

His torch held high, Gloucester rides up to the hut with his thirty soldiers in two dark columns behind. He passes his torch to Kent and hurries to get down from his horse, Kent bringing him over to where the Fool has been charged with steadying the King on his feet.

"What, has Your Grace no better company than this?" Gloucester asks, but Lear is oblivious to the light-hearted teasing.

"The prince of darkness is a gentleman," Edgar snaps indignantly. "Modo he's called, or Mahu some times."

"Our children, my lord," Lear mourns to Gloucester, "have grown so vile they hate us who begot them – "

"Poor Tom's a-cold," Edgar says and looks right at his father.

Taking the torch from Kent, Gloucester points toward the hut.

"Go in with me," he says and takes Lear by the arm. "I can obey your daughters' harsh commands no longer. Though they've ordered me to shut my doors and let you fend for yourself against this storm, yet I have ventured out to find you and bring you to a place where friends await, and fire and food have been made ready."

"First let me talk with this philosopher," Lear protests and puts an arm over Edgar's shoulder. "What is the cause of thunder would you say?"

"Good my Lord," Kent interrupts, "take this offer and go inside."

"First I'll have a word with this learned Greek. What is it you study then?"

"How to thwart the devil and kill vermin," Edgar declares.

"Let me ask you one word in private," says Lear and pulls him aside.

With a helpless look, Kent turns and speaks to Gloucester. "Implore him once again, my lord. His mind is much disturbed."

"No wonder if it's so – his daughters want him dead. Ah," he sighs with a shake of his head, "that good Kent, he said it would be thus, poor banished man. You say the King grows mad? I'll tell thee, friend, I am close to that myself. I had a son, who is outlawed for seeking my life. But I loved him, friend, no father had a dearer son. And speaking true, the grief has hurt my own wits too. What a night this is..." Breaking off, he moves anxiously toward Lear for another try at getting him into the hut. "I do beseech Your Grace – " he says firmly and steps between Edgar and the King.

"But my noble philosopher – his company too," Lear objects.

"Tom's a-cold," Edgar pleads with Gloucester.

"Good, my lord, let him take the fellow," Kent advises.

Gloucester nods impatiently. "Into the hut then and get thee warm." He turns and leads the way. "Come, let's go in," he calls to the others. But in his confusion, Lear heads away from the hut, into the field.

"This way, my Lord – " Kent and the Fool run after him.

"With *him*," the King hollers, pointing to Edgar who has followed Gloucester over to the hut. "I will stay with my philosopher!"

Soldiers ready with Gloucester's bundle of provisions, they light two lanterns from his torch then enter the hut, Kent and the Fool guiding Lear quickly through the door right behind them.

"My good Athenian!" Lear calls back to Edgar.

"No more talk," Gloucester hushes him, passes his torch to a soldier and prepares to go in, but Edgar puts out a hand and stops him.

"Childe Rowland to the dark tower came," he says darkly, "and his words went 'Fee, fie, foh, fum, I smell the blood of a British man…'"

A frowning shake of his head, Gloucester pushes him gently to get inside…

Rain is leaking through the thatched roof in numerous places, though not above the table in the center of the small room where the two lanterns have been placed, affording the hut a dim but welcome light. The Fool doles out the bread, smoked fish and wine that has been brought for them. "Much it is not," Gloucester laments, looking around, "but better than the open air, we must be thankful."

Kent nods. "His mind is overcome with all he's suffered through. The gods reward you for your kindness."

"I go now, but I will not be long in coming again." Shaking hands with Kent, he looks over at Lear, Edgar and the Fool, sitting on milking-stools too low for the table, eating, drinking and being merry like three old friends.…

Standing in the torch-lit hall holding a candle for Edmund while he tries to unlock the door to his father's room, Cornwall is in bad temper. "I will have revenge before I leave this house," he says over Edmund's shoulder.

"I most dread how it will be received that I have chosen loyalty before the bonds of family," Edmund worries, motioning Cornwall to hold the candle closer so he can better see what he's doing. Moments pass but for some reason Edmund can't get the key to work. Exasperated, Cornwall gives him the candle to hold, grabs the key and has no trouble opening the door himself. Edmund smiles weakly, takes back the candle and heads the Duke inside…

"No matter," says Cornwall, "this conduct of your father's – I'm of a mind to think it was in goodness, not for evil, that your brother sought to take his life."

"It may be so, my lord," Edmund concedes, "but sad misfortune it is for me that, in the name of justice, I go against the feelings of my heart… "

In the flickering light of the candle, they move through the darkness toward a writing table on the far side of the room where Edmund lifts the lid on a small wooden chest, sorts through some papers and finds a letter which he reluctantly holds out to Cornwall. "This is where it's proved he aids the King of France, my lord," and a helpless look comes into his face. "By the heavens, I wish his treason were not so, nor I the one to find it out and make it known to you."

Cornwall snatches the letter from him, holds it up to the light and reads. He finishes quickly and looks up. "Go with me to the Duchess," he says and flings the letter at Edmund, but it falls on the floor. He stoops to pick it up.

"If the matter in this letter be true," he ventures, "then you will have mighty business to deal with..."

Cornwall turns and moves toward the door. "True or false, it has made thee Earl of Gloucester. Seek out where your father is that he may be arrested."

"If I find him harboring the King it feeds suspicion to the full," Edmund murmurs under his breath while putting the letter back in the table chest. "I will stay this course of loyalty," he says, turning to Cornwall, "no matter that in doing so, my father will but feel I have forsaken him."

"I trust you well, Edmund," says Cornwall before opening the door. "And in *me*, you will find a dearer father's love…." He passes back the candle, and goes, Edmund watching it burn a moment before he blows it out….

In a corner of the hut where the King has taken refuge, Kent spreads a blanket over the straw bed he has made and rolls up another to serve as a pillow, his eyes glancing frequently over at Lear and Edgar who, with pitchforks in hand, are warily peering at the mounds of straw stored in the shadows at the very back of the room. The Fool is perched cross-legged on the table, comfortably ensconced between the two lanterns and savoring each bite of the apple he is eating.

"The devil Frateretto calls to me," Edgar whispers ominously to Lear. "He tells me Nero is now a fisherman in the hellish lakes below the world." He frowns darkly, turning to Lear and the Fool. "Say your prayers, my simple ones, and beware the fiend who's somewhere near!" He whips his head around and points, beckoning Lear to join him as he jabs and lunges at the shadows.

The Fool looks idly on as, for a few moments, they fight the invisible fiend.

"I wonder, Nuncle," he inquires when they pause to catch their breath. "Would you say a madman is a gentleman or a yeoman?"

"A king, he's a king!" Lear pants, and charges at the piles of straw.

"That may be," the Fool plnders the thought. "He who gave all to his children, and then was all but forgotten…"

" – A thousand flaming arrows come hissing at their heads!" Lear cries, plunging his pitchfork repeatedly into the straw heaps until his arms are too weak to continue and he stops, breathing heavily, exhausted. Edgar comes up beside him and takes the pitchfork away, pointing for Lear to go over and sit down, which he does.

"He's mad who believes in the tameness of wolves," the Fool leans over to tell him. "A horse's health, a whore's promise. Or worst of all," he lowers his voice to a whisper, "a child's love…" Lear, brooding, makes no reply.

"These shall keep the fiend at bay!" Edgar announces and steps away so the others can see the scarecrows he's created in the straw: the pitchforks planted upright, wooden buckets overturned and tilting on their handles.

Lear regards them with a blank stare at first, but then he suddenly erupts. "It shall be done!" He pounds a fist on the table and rises to his feet. "I will arraign them for trial! You," he clutches Edgar, lifts a stool from the floor and slams it on the table. "Come, sit thee here, most learned judge." Edgar takes his appointed place. "You, wise sir, take your seat here." He grabs the Fool and forces him onto a second stool he puts down next to Edgar, then turns with an accusing sneer and addresses the defendants: two pitchforks with wood buckets for heads. "Now, you she-wolves," he says and steps toward them.

"Look how she glares!" Edgar points out from on high, his head almost touching the ceiling. "*Eyes that would frighten the fiend away! Come over Bonnie, and see!*" he cackles in a zany, sing-song voice.

The Fool jumps down from the table and approaches the defendants, folding his arms in mock-serious deliberation as he circles around them. "This Bonnie comes not o'er the ocean," he explains in a firm, judicious voice and points to holes in one of the buckets. "Her boat, it seems, has sprung a leak, and this is why she cannot speak." He turns to Edgar. "She will *not* be coming to thee!" he pronounces conclusively...then breaks into a smile and bows upon receiving Edgar's whistles and wild applause.

But congratulation is short-lived: Edgar suddenly stops clapping and leaps to the ground. A pained and desperate look on his face, he streaks past the pitchforks and disappears in the shadows at the back of the hut where he is violently sick to his stomach.

"The foul fiend haunts Poor Tom in the sweet voice of a nightingale!" he calls out in grim humor when he finishes throwing up. "Hoppedance the devil cries in Tom's belly from the two white herring," he explains hoarsely in the darkness. "Croak not, black angel," he warns, "I've no food left for thee..." When he steps out of the shadows after a few moments, the Fool is waiting with a blanket. Edgar accepts it around his shoulders then looks toward the King: standing before the pitchforks, he stares in quiet amazement at the buckets serving as heads.

"How do you, sir?" Kent asks in some concern, coming up behind. But Lear remains silent, his eyes transfixed. "Be not so bewildered, my Lord," Kent speaks again and puts a gentle hand on Lear's shoulder. "Come, lie down and rest in this bed I have made..."

"I'll see their trial first," Lear declares and, his spirit revitalized, gets down to the business at hand. "Bring in their witnesses," he orders, and gestures to the others. "You, robed man of justice," he calls to Edgar, "back to your place. And you," he says to the Fool, "his partner in justice, up where you belong." Shooing them to their places, he sees Kent looking on. "You are authorized also," he informs him, "so quickly, take your seat."

"Let us deal justly," Edgar announces to the others and, taking the wine bottle from beside him, raps it on the table three times, looking at Lear to begin. "That one first," he growls and points to the pitchfork with a faded gray bucket over its handle. The other bucket is brown.

Edgar nods. "The gray one first," he duly instructs the Fool.

"'Tis Goneril – I swear before this honorable court" Lear says bitterly, " – she who betrayed the poor King her father."

"Step forward, mistress!" the Fool orders. "Is your name Goneril?"

The room is briefly silent.

"She cannot deny it!" Lear scowls. He stalks over to the pitchfork, snatches the gray bucket and, returning it to the table, hands it up to the Fool.

"Mercy's sake," the Fool smirks, "I took you for a bucket."

Lear on his way back to the pitchforks, he lifts off the brown bucket and starts toward the table. "Here is another whose evil looks will show you what her heart is made of," he declares. But Kent is furious: he charges the King, wrests the bucket from him and hurls it into the shadows.

Lear turns fast and puts his hands on a pitchfork. "Over there!" he cries, "stop her!" He lunges forward, swinging and stabbing at the darkness.

Moving swiftly, Kent reaches him from behind, but Lear, at the same moment, wheels to see why no one has come with him – the tines of the pitchfork raking the front of Kent's clothes as the King turns around. "To arms!" he yells in a frenzy, "to arms, swords, fire," he runs at the table and stabs the lanterns, "corruption in the court!" he lunges at the Fool, who dives for safety a mere moment before Kent, using both hands, jerks the pitchfork free and tosses it away.

"Bless thy good wits!" the Fool says, relieved, as Kent struggles on in an effort to restrain the King.

"Treasonous justicer!" Lear flails madly, "why have you let her escape?"

"Pity's sake!" Kent comes back, and shakes him hard, "where is that patience you lately boasted of possessing?"

Pained by the sight, Edgar fights back tears. "I feel his sorrow too much for this pretending," he says to himself and looks away.

"The little dogs and all," Lear pleads with Kent, "Trey, Blanche and Sweetheart, see? They bark at me…" and he points at the darkness.

"Tom will shake his head at them," Edgar cries and comes to stand in position before the King. "*Grrr* and begone you curs!" he snarls through his clenched teeth and makes wild, ferocious movements with his head. "Be your snouts of black or white, teeth that poison if they bite, mastiff, greyhound, mongrel grim, hound or spaniel, her or him – all that wag a dog's tail, Tom will make them weep and wail, by shaking thus his fearsome head – Look!" he cries, "they've leapt the fence and fled. Doe, dee, doe, dee, doe – be off!" He turns and scampers over to Lear, standing beside Kent, his head bowed in defeat. "Come," Edgar invites him, "we'll march to the feasts and all the fairs they're having now in the market towns." He picks up the wine bottle to drink in celebration, but it's empty. "Poor Tom," Edgar pouts, "his bottle's dry…"

"Let them dissect Regan then," Lear grumbles. "See what breeds inside her heart, see why nature made that heart so cold…" He notices Edgar still beside him. "You, sir," he says and places his arm on the madman's shoulder. "I include you now in my hundred, only I do not like the fashion of your clothes." Edgar looks down at his nearly naked body. "For you they may be handsome, but let them be changed…" He wavers as though dizzy, his eyes fluttering closed.

"Good my Lord," Kent says and catches him, "lie down and rest awhile."

Lear lets himself be helped over to the straw bed. "No noise," he whispers with a finger to his lips, "no noise…" Kent and the Fool lower him onto the bed. "Draw the curtains," he murmurs, his head reaching the blanket pillow. "So, so, so…" he mutters peacefully, the Fool tucking him in. "We'll go to supper in the morning," Lear smiles.

"And I'll go to bed at noon," the Fool answers gently.

"So, so, so…" He smiles at the Fool once more, closes his eyes and falls fast asleep.

Kent returns to the table where, heaving a weary sigh, he sits down. The Fool is about to join him when he notices something different about the hut. He glances around, goes over and whistles in the darkness, but there's no sign of Poor Tom. He alerts Kent who only shrugs, too tired to be concerned right now. Still, the Fool decides it's worth a look outside, motions Kent to that effect and is starting for the door when it swings open suddenly and Gloucester comes rushing in, desperate and distraught.

"Where is the King my master?" he demands and darts his eyes around the hut.

Kent gets quickly to his feet, a finger to his lips for silence. "Here, sir," he points to the straw bed in the corner, "but trouble him not, his wits are gone."

Gloucester takes a quick look then turns to Kent. "Good friend, I pray you," he urges, hushing his voice and speaking fast, "get him up and away from here. I have overheard a plot to have him killed. There is a wagon ready outside. Lay him in it and drive toward Dover, where you shall receive both welcome and protection. Get your master up and away, friend: if you should dally half an hour his life, and yours, and all who are ready to defend him, will assuredly be lost. Get him up, I say, and come with me at once."

He follows Kent and the Fool over to the bed, peers down with them at the King.

Kent deliberates uneasily. "His troubled spirit sleeps," he says. "This rest might yet relieve the shaken nerves in him." He weighs the distress in Gloucester's face. "But, if we cannot get him the help he needs, and soon, the prospects for his recovery are slim." Gloucester nods. "Come," Kent orders the Fool, "help me carry your master."

"I tell you, there is not a moment to spare," Gloucester warns and readies himself to help with the King…

Outside, where the rain has slowed to no more than a drizzle, Edgar appears from around the side of the hut, crawling forward on his hands and knees until he can see more clearly what's going on: a covered wagon and Gloucester's mounted troops are waiting in front of the door, jumping into action when Gloucester's voice goes up inside.

Soldiers bring a litter from the back of the wagon and set it down in front of the door, Kent and the Fool emerging in a few moments with the King, an arm around each of their shoulders but still sound asleep.

Gloucester following with the blankets, he directs the careful lowering of Lear onto the litter, sees it lifted quickly into the back of the wagon, then waves Kent and the Fool to climb in after. Helped on his horse, he signals to the soldier driving the wagon, and the retinue, bound for Dover, rides out, Gloucester turning his horse in the opposite direction to return to his castle.

Edgar stays out of sight even after they've gone, ruminating on events of the last few hours. "When we behold our betters bearing our woes," he reflects, "hard it is to see our own miseries as foes. Who suffers alone, suffers most in the mind, leaving carefree things and happier thoughts behind. But then the mind much suffering can endure, if grief has company, the fellowship of friends to cure. How easy, light and bearable my private pain seems now, when that which makes me bend, makes the good King bow. His children driving him, as my father did me, away, heed rumors in high places, Tom, yourself the madman stay, until the lies and misconceptions that defiled thee, are proved unjust, and truth with your accusers reconciles thee. Lurk, lurk," he chants warily, gets to his feet and slips away into the night....

The stone hearth in Gloucester's private meeting room is almost as tall as Cornwall. He gazes into the fire, flames beginning to snap and blaze around the fresh logs with which it's just been stoked, and listens while Regan, seated at the long oak table behind him, finishes reading the letter found in Gloucester's room. "*'As well, it is confirmed from France there comes a force who in our coastal ports have gained a foothold, and are almost at the point of making known the cause they*

fight for is the saving of our King.' Hang him instantly," she says, looking up.

"Pluck out his eyes!" says Goneril, hovering behind her sister.

Edmund, standing nearby, says nothing.

"Leave him to my devices," Cornwall rules, and turns from the fire. He signals across the torch-lit room to a train of soldiers, the officer in charge quickly coming over. "Seek out the traitor Gloucester," Cornwall orders. "Bring him before us. Go." The officer bows, motions for his men to follow and rushes from the room. "Meantime, my sister Goneril, make haste to my lord your husband and show him the letter. Edmund, go you with her: whatever our revenge upon your traitorous father, it is not fit for your beholding. Advise Albany to prepare for war with utmost speed. We shall do likewise. Messengers conveying news can swiftly pass between us as together we make ready to defend against invasion. Farewell, dear sister. Farewell, my lord of Gloucester."

Goneril looks to Edmund and confers a smile of pleased congratulation, as does Regan when she gets up from the table to hand back Gloucester's letter.

"What news, where's the King?" Cornwall demands when he sees Oswald coming into the room.

"Some thirty of my lord of Gloucester's knights have taken him to Dover," the steward reports, "where they boast of having many well-armed friends."

The news not to his liking, Cornwall glowers. "Ready the horses for your mistress," he tells Oswald, "and our Duke of Gloucester," he quickly adds.

Oswald bows to Cornwall then Goneril, Regan, and now Edmund, venturing a smile at the new Duke of Gloucester which is most politely returned…

"Farewell, sweet lord and sister," Goneril says, embracing Regan then Cornwall when he comes over.

"Farewell, sister," Cornwall replies, turning to Edmund beside her. "Farewell, my lord of Gloucester…

Goneril's train of attendants falling in, she and Edmund depart, Gloucester's frightened servants bowing as they pass.

"Find your master," Cornwall yells at them from across the room. "Bind him like a thief and bring him before us." The servants promptly scurry for the door, Cornwall returning to the hearth where he takes up a black iron poker and stirs the fire.

"Though we may not pass sentence on his life without a proper trial," he muses aloud to Regan, "still it is within our power to let our wrath be known, which some will fault us for, but none may challenge."

A noise of scuffling and commotion goes up in the hall outside the chamber.

"Is that the traitor?" Cornwall demands. His guard officer marches in, soldiers holding Gloucester by the arms behind him.

"Ungrateful fox, it's him," Regan says with disdain.

"Bind fast his withered arms."

"What is the meaning of this, your graces," Gloucester asks as he's taken over and planted on a chair. "Good my friends, remember: you are my guests. Do me no foul play."

"Bind him, I say – " Cornwall orders, a rope is brought and Gloucester's arms tied together behind the back of the chair.

"Hard," Regan says and goes over, tightening the rope herself. "Filthy traitor," she says scornfully and looks down at Gloucester, pinioned to the chair.

"Merciless lady that you are, I am no traitor," he declares proudly.

Cornwall strikes the poker against the stone hearth. "Villain! You shall find – "

But Regan pulls at his wispy beard.

"By the kind gods," Gloucester winces as she tears out some hair, "'Tis shameful you would do this."

"So white," Regan holds up the hair, "yet such a dark traitor."

"Wicked woman, these hairs you rip from my chin will come to life and condemn thee. I am your host," he repeats. "With robber's hands my favor and generosity you should not abuse as roughly as you do. What do you intend?"

"Come, sir," Cornwall questions, "what letters had you recently from France?"

"Be clear in your answers, for we know the truth."

"And what alliance have you," Cornwall continues, "with the traitors who have set foot in our kingdom?"

" – To whose hands you have sent the lunatic King," Regan adds. "Speak."

Gloucester strains uncomfortably in the chair. "I have a letter containing speculations from one who's of a neutral heart, neither for nor opposed."

"Most cunning," says Cornwall with a bitter smirk.

"And a lie," Regan snaps.

"Where have you sent the King?"

"To Dover."

"Why to Dover?" Regan demands. "Were you not ordered on pain of death – "

"Why to Dover?" Cornwall cuts in. "Let him tell us that."

Gloucester lifts his chin nobly. "Like a beast, I am tied to the stake and must stand the course of your baiting," he says, refusing them an answer.

"Why to Dover, sir?" Regan shouts close to his face.

He stares up at her. "Because I would not see your cruel nails pluck out his poor old eyes," he says placidly. "Nor your vicious sister sink her serpent fangs in his anointed, kingly flesh. The sea, with such a storm as his bare head in hell-black night endured, would have risen up and drowned the fiery stars, yet, poor old heart, he defied the heavens to rain their worst and take his life, but they could not. If wolves had at your gate been howling in piteous misery you would have said 'Good porter, let the animals in.' But a man, you gave no such compassion… No, I shall see heaven's vengeance fall – that children could treat a father so."

"See it you never shall, old man," Cornwall says, grabbing him by the hair.

"He who would live till he be old, give me some help – " he pleads, but Cornwall drives the iron poker in his eye. "O cruel – O you gods!" he shrieks, his body jolting with the pain.

"The other one too," Regan urges.

"You wish to see vengeance – " He raises the poker to strike but the guard officer steps forward and stays his hand.

"Stop, my lord! I have served you ever since I was a boy, but better service never have I done than bid you now to hold."

"What's this, you dog?" Regan turns on him in a fury.

"If you had a beard upon your face I would believe it," the officer condemns her. "How dare you do this?"

"Speak thus, thou servant?" Cornwall rages and lashes the officer's face with the poker.

The officer stumbles back, drawing his sword. "Come, sir, you can do better than that," he taunts and charges Cornwall, whose blade is out and swinging as they clash. The officer a hard and more masterful fighter, he lunges when Cornwall is off balance and runs him through with his sword.

"Give me thy blade!" Regan shouts and grabs a nearby soldier's weapon. "A peasant stand up thus?" She runs at him from behind and plunges the sword in his back.

"I'm slain," he cries out, staggering toward Gloucester. "My lord, you have one eye left – to see some justice d – " but before he can finish he falls to the floor, groans briefly and dies.

Clutching the wound in his chest, Cornwall struggles to retrieve the poker then turns and brutally gouges Gloucester's other eye. "Out, vile jelly! Where is thy luster now?"

"All dark and comfortless?" Gloucester moans in utter despair. "Where's my son Edmund?" he pleads. "Edmund, fan your feelings into flame and avenge this horrible act…"

"Ha! You treacherous villain," Regan mocks, "you call upon one who hates thee – it was he who is too good to pity thee that made known your conspiracy to us."

Gloucester groans as the truth dawns. "O my blind folly! Then Edgar was wronged from the beginning… Kind gods, forgive me for what I have done. Let him prosper wherever he may be."

"Go, throw him out at the gates and let him smell his way to Dover."

Gloucester's servants are brought in to untie him, Regan rushing to Cornwall who slumps bleeding in a chair. "How is it, my lord…"

"I am wounded, that is all." He gets to his feet, a hand on the table to steady himself, and makes his way across the chamber. "Turn out that eyeless villain!" he shouts to other servants entering the room. Toss the slave upon the dung heap! Regan, I bleed badly. Untimely comes this hurt. Give me your arm…" She puts her arm around him and helps him from the room, his servants doing the same for Gloucester who follows slowly behind.

"I cannot care what wickedness I ever do if this man come to good," one of the servants whispers bitterly.

"If she lives long and dies a natural death, women will all become monsters," the other servant says.

"Let's stay with the old Earl and get the vagabond beggar to lead him where he can. His wild madness allows him to wander freely."

They reach the door, guiding Gloucester into the torch-lit hall. "Go with him," the first servant says. "I'll fetch some linseed and whites of eggs to help his bleeding eyes. The heavens be with him now!"

They go their separate directions, the servant who stays with Gloucester humming to him in a gentle voice as they slowly move along….

4.1

A once lofty oak tree, struck by lightning during the previous night's storm, has toppled onto a bridge: the only way over the rushing waters of the rain-swollen river now, is along the tree's thick trunk, where, close to the middle, Edgar sits brooding. " ...Better despised as the beggar I've become," he reflects, gazing down at the water, "than one in power who is despised but must be flattered. Being now among the lowest, most helpless and dejected, is not the worst that could be," he ventures, but breaks off and gets quickly to his feet when he notices a gray rabbit stranded on the back of an overturned cart the eddying current is bearing swiftly downstream.

He watches for a moment, gauging when the cart will arrive beneath him, the petrified rabbit wet and trembling on the floating cart as it verges quickly closer. Picking a position where he will enter the water, he waits a moment then jumps. He plunges in and goes under, the current whisking him rapidly forward as he surfaces, arms reaching to grab the moving cart by one of its handles. He talks soothingly to the animal and kicks his feet, veering into shallow water where he takes the terrified creature in his arms and carries it to shore, resuming his reflection as he goes.

" ...No, there is always hope when things are at their worst," he says gamely. "This lamentable change in fortune is already for the best, since the worst can now be glimpsed behind. And laughed at," he says, walking up from the water and into the woods where he sets the rabbit down, nudging gently with his foot to get it hopping which it presently starts to do. Watching as it disappears in the leafy undergrowth, he breathes deeply and returns to his thoughts of a few minutes before. "Welcome, thou winds of change," he declares boldly and peers up at the surrounding trees. "This wretch you have cast down as low as man could ever be, has nothing left to fear from thee." He looks in several directions, but finally decides on the forest straight ahead and starts walking, only to discover, before he has gone far, that others are in the woods this morning too…

His face brown and weathered from a life toiling in the farm fields, an old man brings Gloucester haltingly along the forest path, the holes that were his eyes still oozing blood, his bruised face buzzing with flies that have caught the scent.

Close by, watching them through the trees as they walk, Edgar recoils when he recognizes his father. "World, world, O world," he moans. "If thy monstrous nature did not astound and make us hate thee, life would not give in with such solace to old age and death…"

"But my good lord," the old man is pleading with Gloucester, " I have been your follower and your father's follower for nigh on eighty years."

Gloucester stops walking and lets go of his hand. "Get thee away from me, good friend. Be gone. Your help can do me no good whatsoever – indeed, it can but bring you harm, since it is forbidden that any should assist me."

"But my good sir," the old man protests, "you cannot see where you are going."

"There *is* nowhere I am going," Gloucester comes back, "and therefore I need no eyes: I stumbled when I saw." He waves a hand blindly at the flies around his face. "Too often we are so confident in the comforts of prosperity we do not see what a blessing our afflictions can be." He sighs wistfully. "O dear son Edgar, victim of thy father's mistaken anger, if I could only live long enough to reach out my hands and touch you, I could feel what it is to have my sight again."

Looking on from the bushes beside the path, Edgar groans in such distress that the old man glances over.

"Who's there?" he demands.

"O you gods," Edgar despairs, ducking out of sight. "How can I say I have reached the worst? I am worse off than ever I was – "

" 'Tis poor mad Tom," the old man informs Gloucester.

" – And worse I yet may find myself," Edgar continues, "but things are not the very worst when I can gaze upon this dismal sight and say '*This* is the worst that could ever be.'"

The old man glimpses Edgar through the leaves. "Fellow!" he calls, "where are you heading?"

"Is it a beggar man?" Gloucester asks.

"That, and a madman too."

"Yet he must have some good sense if he knows enough to beg," Gloucester remarks. "In the storm last night I saw such a fellow, one who made me think a man no better than the merest bug. For some reason I was reminded of my son, even though I had hatefully put all thoughts of him from my mind. But I have learned more since: as flies to mischievous boys are we to the gods, they torment us for their amusement."

"What can I do?" Edgar agonizes. "Worthless is he to himself and others who would play the mad fool with one in such sorrow." He thinks for a moment. "Bless thee, master!" he says and steps out from behind the trees.

"Is that the naked fellow?" Gloucester turns in the direction of Edgar's voice.

"Yes, my lord."

"I beseech you," Gloucester tells the old man, "be on your way then, and for the sake of our old friendship meet us a mile or two hence, closer to Dover, with some apparel for this naked soul, who I'll entreat to lead me in the meanwhile."

"But sir, he is mad," the old man protests.

" 'Tis the sickness of our time that madmen must lead the blind," Gloucester says mournfully. "Do what I ask you, friend, or if not, for your own good be gone."

"I'll bring him the best garments I have," the old man declares with resolve, exchanging looks with Edgar before he moves off on the forest path.

"Are you there, naked fellow?"

Edgar hesitates, torn as to what he should do. "Poor Tom's a-cold," he blurts finally, but can't bring himself to say more. "Play this mad part I will no longer – "

"Come here, fellow."

" – And yet I must," Edgar tells himself, now that he sees the gruesome state of his father's face more clearly. " – Bless thy sweet eyes, they bleed," he says tenderly and comes to stand in front of his father.

"Do you know the way to Dover, fellow?"

"From pillar to post, each footpath and roadway," Edgar answers then makes an ominous moan. "But Poor Tom has been scared out of his good wits by the foul fiend! Beware of him, good-man sir," he warns. "His wily demons will possess you – five have been in Poor Tom and all at one time, that was Obidicut, to make him lust, Hobbididence, prince of darkness, Mahu, who steals, Modo, who murders, Flibbertigibbet, who pouts and makes scolding faces – who since possesses young maids and old wives it is said. So watch yourself, master, is what I say."

"You take this purse then," Gloucester says, moved to sympathy, "you whom heaven's plagues have taught to bear your miseries so humbly." Gloucester withdraws a small pouch from under his cloak and holds it out. "Why shouldn't I make thee the happier," Gloucester demands, "now that I am one of the wretched?" He shakes the purse insistently until Edgar takes it from him. "And the heavens keep it ever so!" Gloucester proclaims, seizing his son's hands and clutching them in his own. "Let the man steeped in luxury and abundance, who feeds his every selfish whim in defiance of your heavenly will – who cannot see the needs of others because he does not feel them himself – O you heavens," he prays solemnly, "let him feel your power sharply now: and let all who have too much, be forced to share with those who have too little, so that each man has enough of what he needs." He sighs and stays quiet for some moments. "Do you know Dover?" he asks Edgar presently.

"Yes master, I do."

"There is a high cliff that overhangs the sea most far below. Bring me but to the very brim of it, and I'll relieve thee of thy misery with something of great value I have upon me." He pauses. "From there I shall no leading need…"

"Give me your arm, master," Edgar says fondly. "Poor Tom shall lead thee." He turns his father in the right direction and arm in arm they start along the path....

Having ridden all night and through the morning, the troops escorting Goneril wait restlessly on their horses for the gates of her palace to open, Edmund, beside the princess, gazing up with interest at the Duke of Albany's flag, waving in the wind above the lofty stone towers.

"Welcome, my lord." Goneril smiles over from her horse. Edmund meets her eyes but says nothing: a commotion has gone up in front of the gate. There is a problem with the chain-wheel, which is preventing the great wooden doors from opening more than a crack that is only wide enough for a person to fit through. The party will have to leave their horses and enter the palace on foot. Shouts and raised voices from the tired soldiers in reply, Edmund helps Goneril down from her horse and the two of them lead the way inside.

"I wonder that my husband should so forget his manners not to greet us," she remarks as they enter the castle yard where Oswald, greatly disconcerted, rushes immediately forward so he will be first to speak with his lady.

"Well," she demands, "where's your master?"

"Within, madam. But never have I seen a man so changed. When I told him of the army that had landed, he smiled at the news. I let him know you were coming and he answered 'So much the worse.' Of Gloucester's treason and the loyalty shown by his son," he looks to Edmund, "I informed him too, only to be cursed as a fool and repugnantly dismissed. What he should dislike pleases him, what he should like, he finds offensive."

Goneril broods for a moment before drawing Edmund aside. "Then you shall go no further," she tells him. "It's the cowardly fear he has of committing to a cause," she says with disdain. "He'd swallow any number of wrongs before he'd ever stand up and defend his rights." She steps closer to him. "The wishes we talked of on our way here may find themselves fulfilled," she whispers into his ear then turns so others within the yard can hear. "Back, Edmund, to my brother. Hasten the mustering of his troops and command them against these enemies…"

She puts her arm in his and walks him back to the gate. "For now I must change names and be the master of this house, while he behaves like its mistress," she complains in bitter sarcasm. "But meantime my trusted steward will bring messages between us."

They arrive at the crack in the gate. "And I promise," she says, "it won't be long before you hear – if you are willing to seek your heart's desire – from a future wife." She takes off the chain medallion she wears around her neck. "Have this." Edmund starts to speak but she closes his mouth with a finger. "Bow your head." He does, and she slips on the chain. "This kiss, if it could speak, would raise you up for all the world to see." She touches her lips to his. "Remember…and fare you well."

"Yours in the ranks of death," he says, and returns the kiss.

" – Most dear Gloucester," she whispers. A parting smile, he bows and slips through the opening in the gate. "O the difference of one man from another," she says as he walks over and mounts his horse. "To you a woman's embraces are due. Here an undeserving fool shares my bed – "

"Madam, my lord is coming," Oswald warns from behind her.

A last look at Edmund, Goneril turns and moves to meet her husband. "There was a time when I was worth a welcome home."

"Goneril, you are not worth the dust the rude wind blows in your face. I fear the lengths to which you would go in pursuing these despisèd ends. There is no restraining you, no telling what your limits might be. I do know, however, that cutting yourself off from your father as you have done, as a branch tears itself from the tree that has given it life and sustained it – "

"No more," she snaps in objection, "this is nothing but foolish nonsense."

"Wisdom and goodness to the vile seem vile," he continues. "The filthy savor the taste of their own filth. What have you done? You are tigers, not daughters. What horrors have you a mind to perform? A father, a gracious and revered old man – in whose presence even a dog-baited, snarling bear would gently settle – you have most barbarously and degenerately driven mad. Could my brother stand by and allow this? A man, a prince who has benefited so much by him? If the heavens will not send quickly down avenging spirits to punish these vile offences, it is only a matter of time. Humanity will prey upon itself like monsters of the deep."

"You feeble man," she mocks. "Your cheek ever turning the other to blows, your ear deaf to insults, your eye blind to the difference between honor which must be defended, and suffering in noble silence. None but fools take pity on those villains who are punished before they can do further harm. Where's the sound of your drum? France unfurls his banners and with helmeted battalions threatens the peace in our land, while you, a moralizing fool, sit and cry 'Alas, why does he so?'"

"Look at yourself, devil. The ugliness of the fiend is never so hideous as when it shows in the pleasing shape of a woman."

"You driveling fool," she sneers and makes a face.

"You have hidden your nature well, fiend," he comes back. "But no matter your disgusted looks, you cannot become more monstrous than you already are. If it were my way, and you were not a fiend disguised in a woman's body, I would let these hands obey their feelings and tear you limb from limb and to pieces after that."

"My, my, what manhood," she scoffs bitterly. "*Mew!*" she purrs.

Looking over her shoulder, he watches through the gate where a rider has appeared. The man jumps down from his horse, takes something from his saddlebag and rushes forward to speak with Albany.

"What news?"

"O my good lord, the Duke of Cornwall's dead, slain by his servant while going to put out the other eye of Gloucester."

"Gloucester's eyes?"

The messenger nods. "One who he raised from boyhood, struck with compassion for the old man, stopped his hand before the act and turned his sword on his master, who flew at him fiercely and in the fight thereafter felled him dead, but not before receiving the wound that has since killed him."

"This shows you are above, you heavenly powers, that the crimes of this world so swiftly are avenged. But poor Gloucester, lost he his other eye?"

"Both my lord, yes." He turns to Goneril. "This letter, madam, demands a speedy answer. 'Tis from your sister." He bows and hands it to her.

"I'll read and give you an answer," she says, moving past Albany and across the castle yard.

"One way I like this well the death of Cornwall," she says as she goes, "although it leaves my Gloucester with his widow," she reasons, "which may send the dreams my heart is building crashing down and leave me in this hateful life I have." She walks faster approaching the door, which a servant hurries to open. "But in other ways the news is not so grim," she muses and goes in…

"Where was his son while they were taking his eyes?" Albany asks, turning back to the messenger.

"Come hither with my lady."

"But he is not here."

"No, my good lord. I met him heading back."

"He knows about this wickedness?"

"Indeed, my lord, 'twas he informed against his father and quit the house on purpose that their punishment might have the freer course."

"Gloucester," Albany mourns, "I will live to thank thee for this love thou showed'st the King and to revenge the eyes you've lost." He points outside the gate. "Bring your horse and tell me what else thou knows't," he instructs the messenger, then signals to the keeper of his gate and watches while the doors swing slowly open.…

In the rear of the French army camp near Dover, Kent sits between several unused baggage carts listening to the soldier he met during the storm, some disconcerting news he's just received prompting him to a troubled shake of his head.

"Know you *why* the King has suddenly gone back to France?"

"Something he was forced to leave unresolved at the time he left to come here, is what they say," the soldier replies, "but which has plunged his kingdom into such fear that it necessitates his return."

"What general has he given the command of his army?"

"The Marshall of France, Monsieur la Far."

Kent purses his lips and nods, familiar with the name. "Did the letters you delivered move the queen to any demonstration of grief?" he asks after a moment.

"Yes, sir. She took them, read them in my presence, and several times the tears slipped down her cheeks, but she was a queen over her feelings, which fought to be king over her."

"It moved her then to hear of him?"

The soldier nods. "But not to anger. Patience and sorrow vied together over who could make her appear most beautiful. If you've seen it shower rain when the sun is still shining?" Kent nods. "This was more lovely. The happy smiles that played upon her lips seemed not to know of the watery guests in her eyes, which slipped away like pearls from diamonds dropped. Sorrow would be something precious and sought after if it brought to others what it did to her."

"Did she question you?"

"Once or twice she uttered her father's name, but choked on the word as if it weighed too heavily upon her heart to think of him. Cried 'Sisters, sisters, shameless sisters! Kent, father, sisters! Let it for pity not be believed!' Thereupon she shook with sobs, tears mixing with her sorrowful cries, and she turned away from me to deal with her grief alone."

"It is the stars," Kent says, "the stars above which govern the state of things. Else a man and woman could never beget such wholly different children," he declares. "You spoke not with her since?"

"No."

"Was this before her husband left for France?"

"No, after."

"Well, sir, the poor distressed Lear's in Dover as we speak, remembering in his better moments why we've come, but he will not agree to see his daughter."

"Good sir, why not?"

"He's wracked with shame," Kent says and looks away. "His own unkindness that stripped her of his blessing and sent her away to fend for herself in a foreign land, giving her substantial rights and property to his dog-hearted daughters. These things sting his mind so venomously the shame burns inside him for how she was so wronged."

"Alas, the poor man."

Kent gets to his feet. "Of Albany's and Cornwall's powers you heard not?"

"Indeed, sir, they are on the march," the soldier says uneasily as he rises.

"Well, then, I'll bring you to our master, Lear, and leave you to attend him. There is one important matter yet for me to deal with, sir, thus my name must be concealed a while longer. When who I am can finally be revealed, you will not rue the friendship and assistance you have shown. Pray you, let us go."

They step out from behind the wagons, hurry through the camp and into the nearby woods....

After checking the contents of a covered basket he's carrying, the guards stationed outside Cordelia's tent make way for the elderly, learned-looking man in the cap and robes of a doctor. The flap held open for him, he goes inside.

" 'Tis he," Cordelia agrees with the officer standing across from her at a table spread with papers, maps and battle plans. She nods a greeting to the doctor, waving him forward to join them. "He was seen just now," she says, "mad as the storming sea, singing aloud, covered in burdocks, twigs and nettles, with a wreath of wildflowers crowning his head." The doctor smiles thoughtfully and sets his basket on the table. Cordelia turns to the officer. "Send out a hundred men to look for him," she instructs. "Search every acre in all the surrounding fields until you find him." When the officer has departed she comes out from behind the table to stand with the doctor..

"I pray your science will do whatever it can to restore him to his right mind," she says, her voice concerned but hopeful. "He that cures him shall have all that I own in this world," she says solemnly.

"There is a way, madam," he advises, "but nature's best nurse is rest, in which he is bound to be severely lacking. To bring that on are various excellent healing herbs, whose effects will gently close his anguished eyes." He lifts the cover on the basket to let her view the flowers inside.

She reaches in and takes a sprig in her hand, lifts and touches it to her cheek. "All your healing secrets flourish with my tears," she urges, "and find a way to cure the good man's cruel distress...before his raving madness kills the power of reason to assuage it."

A call goes up outside, the tent door is pulled open and a messenger rushes in. "News, madam," he announces, and approaches the table. "The British armies are making toward us."

"So we have heard," she acknowledges calmly. "We are prepared and ready." She nods to him and he goes quickly out, the doctor following after. " – O dear father," she says, "it is your business that I embark upon. This is why great France has taken pity on my mournful and persistent pleas. No other bold ambition has incited us to take up arms, but *love*, precious love, and the justness of an aged father's cause: soon may I hear and see him again...."

Regan is seated by the fire in her room at Gloucester's castle, turning a handkerchief in her hands while Oswald stands beside her chair dutifully waiting for her to speak.

"But are my brother Albany's troops sent forth?" she finally asks.

"They are, madam."

"Himself in person leading them?"

"Reluctant and with much persuasion, yes." Then adds: "Your sister is the better soldier."

She thinks a moment.

"Lord Edmund spoke not with your lord at home?"

"No, madam."

"What does my sister's letter to him say?" she asks, looking up.

"I know not, my lady."

She considers. "Well, he has sped off on some urgent matter. It was a mistake, Gloucester's eyes being out, to let him live," she complains. "Wherever he goes all hearts are moved against us." She reflects. "Edmund, pitying the old man's pain I suppose, has gone to put him out of his misery…as well as discover the enemy's strength," she adds, but absently.

" – I must needs go after him with my letter, madam," Oswald says, eager to be going.

"Our troops set forth tomorrow. Why not stay here the night, with us. The roads are dangerous too."

"I cannot, madam," he replies. "My lady gave me strictest orders in this business."

"Why should she *write* to Edmund. Might not her plans be sent by word of mouth?" She regards the handkerchief between her hands. "But I suppose," she continues, "some small thing, I don't know what – " She gets to her feet and faces him. "I'll value thee much: let me unseal the letter."

"Madam, I had rather – " he takes a step back.

"I know your lady does not love her husband, I'm sure of it," she presses him, "and when last she was here, gave Edmund furtive glances and clearly amorous looks. I know she takes you in her confidence."

"I, madam?"

"It is no *secret* to me. She does, I know it." She turns and looks at the fire. "Therefore take note of this: my lord is dead. Edmund and I have talked, and more suitable is he for my hand than your lady's." She waves her fingers at him. "Gather the rest as you will…and if you do find him," she carries on, "pray you give him this." She holds out her handkerchief. He nods, smiling, and accepts it. "And when your mistress hears as much from you, pray, tell her to come to her senses. So, fare you well." He bows to her and goes, but she calls across the room: "If you hear by chance of that blind traitor, promotion lies in store for the man that sends him to it…"

Oswald stops walking and turns. "If I were to meet him, madam," he declares, "I would show him whose side I am on."

"Farewell…" When he's gone, she returns to her chair and goes back to watching the fire….

Dressed in peasant's clothing now, Edgar carries his father on his back toward the bottom of a wide, gently sloping field, Gloucester's frail arms holding tight to his son's shoulders as they go along.

"When shall I come to the top of that same cliff?" he wonders.

"You do climb up it now," Edgar tells him. "Look how we labor."

"Methinks the ground is flat."

"Horrible steep," Edgar huffs and strains his voice. "Listen. Can't you hear the sea?"

"No, truly I cannot."

"Why then, your other senses are made faulty by the anguish of your eyes."

"Indeed, it must be so." He listens again, but only hears Edgar's puffing breath. "Methinks your voice has changed and you speak in a different way than you did before."

"You're much mistaken, sir. Nothing has changed but my garments."

"Methinks you are better spoken," Gloucester insists.

"Come on, sir, here's the place…"

Edgar slows down as though moving precariously toward the edge of a towering ocean cliff…though in fact he has reached the top of an embankment that gives onto a dry streambed, numerous trees from the oak forest on the opposite side having toppled onto the pebbled beach between the two embankments, some during the recent storm, others over the passing years. "No further than this," he warns and lets out a breath.

"How it makes one dizzy to gaze far below: the ravens that glide through the air but half way down the cliff look small and black as beetles. The fishermen that walk upon the beach appear like mice, and yon tall anchored ship no larger than a rowing boat my eyes can hardly see. The murmuring surf that washes the line of shore cannot be heard from here. I'll look no more," he says anxiously and steps back, "lest my head start spinning and dizziness send us headlong from this precipice to our death – "

"Set me down."

Edgar crouches and lets his father slide from his back. "Give me your hand," he cautions. "You are now within a foot of the very edge. For nothing under the sun would I stand so close – "

"Let go of my hand," Gloucester says and, reaching inside his blood-blackened coat, withdraws a leather pouch, which he holds out to Edgar. "Here, friend, is another purse for thee, in it a jewel well worth a poor man's taking. With the help of the gods may you thrive and ever prosper." Edgar takes the pouch. "Now stand you back. Bid me farewell and let me hear you going."

Edgar cups his hands around his mouth. "Fare you well then, good sir," he hollers as if from a distance.

"The same to you with all my heart!"

"If I play upon his despair perhaps I will cure it," Edgar muses to himself as he watches his father kneel and fold his hands in prayer.

"O you mighty gods, this world I now abandon, and in your sight shake patiently my great affliction off. If I could bear it longer and not fall to quarrel with your firm and constant wills, my useless and despisèd life would not be so snuffed out, but burn more gradually down unto its purposed end. If Edgar lives, bless him!" He keeps his head bowed for a moment then gets to his feet. "Now, fellow, fare you well!" he calls to Edgar, raises his chin nobly and falls forward…

"Goodbye, sir. Farewell," Edgar answers, peering at his father's motionless body at the foot of the embankment not far below. "And yet for all we know," he reflects, making his way down the bank, "it may be in the mind that we are robbed of treasured life, if the body itself does give so readily up." He reaches the streambed where Gloucester is lying face down on the stones. "Had he been where he thought, all would be over with by now," he says sadly, and rolls his father onto his back. He waits a moment longer then begins patting his father's cheeks. "Dead or alive?" he asks in a different sounding voice.

"Ho, you sir!" He puts his face closer. "Friend, can you hear me? Speak, sir!" There is no sign of life in the old man. "Perhaps he died after all," Edgar says, but notices Gloucester stirring. "Yet he revives. What are you, sir?"

"Go away and let me die," Gloucester grumbles.

"Had you been anything but gossamer, feathers or mist, falling so many fathoms down you would have smashed to pieces like an egg. But still you breathe, your body is not broken, there is no blood, and you can speak. Ten masts end to end would not reach that height from which you plummeted, yet by some miracle you have survived. Speak again."

"But have I fallen or not?"

"From the mighty summit of this chalk cliff," Edgar exclaims. "Gaze up: the shrill-voiced lark cannot be seen or heard so far away. Look up, sir."

"Alas, I have no eyes," Gloucester confesses and sits up. "Has a wretched man not the right to end his own life?" he demands bitterly. " 'Twas the only hope in the midst of misery, the thought of foiling even a tyrant's rage by doing so…"

"Give me your arm," Edgar says and helps his father to his feet. "How is it? Feel you your legs?"

"Too well, too well," Gloucester laments.

"This is beyond all strangeness," Edgar says, pretending amazement. "Tell me, at the top of the cliff, what thing was that which parted from you a moment before you leaped?

"A poor unfortunate beggar, sir."

"As I stood here below, methought his eyes were two full moons. He had a thousand tentacle noses, horns that spiraled out of his head, and hideous, jutting jaws. It was some fiend, I think," he says ominously. "Therefore, most happy father, you have somehow been saved by the gracious gods above, whose glory is doing that for us which is truly and fully miraculous."

"I do remember now," Gloucester nods then stays quiet for a moment. "Henceforth I will bear with my affliction till it cries out 'Enough, enough' and dies of its own accord. That thing you speak of," he returns to Edgar's question, "I took it for a man. Often it would cry 'The fiend, the fiend.' It was he who led me to that place from which I jumped," he says, and heaves a tired sigh.

"May your thoughts be less dark and troubled from now forward," Edgar says to console him, noticing a moment later that a man has rolled down the far bank. Getting up from the stones, he starts walking toward them: head down and talking to himself as his feet crunch the stones, Lear's ragged clothes are stuck with burrs and nettles. Twigs are sticking out of his long white hair, in which he's poked and tied wildflowers.

"They cannot call counterfeit! I am the King himself. A born king is above the law. He needs no bribes. The way that fellow handled his bow he wouldn't scare off crows. Draw the arrow back, sir, right to your ear. Look, look, a mouse!" He starts running to try and catch it, but stops suddenly. "Calm down old man. This piece of toasted cheese will do it." He pretends he's eating. "That's my challenge, sir, and I'll stand by it even against a giant. But show the weapons." He swings an imaginary sword, pulls back the string of a bow. "*Hewgh!* " he releases an arrow. "Bull's eye, bull's eye! *Hewgh!*" he shouts in Edgar's face. Then, after a sly look to either side, he puts his face even closer to Edgar's and whispers: "What's the word?"

"Marjoram," Edgar whispers back.

Lear nods and makes way. "Pass."

"I know that voice," Gloucester says, perking up.

"Ha!" Lear cries and turns on him. "Goneril, with a white beard? They flattered me like fawning dogs and raved about my wisdom, went 'yes' and 'no' to every word I said till neither mattered much. Yet when the rain came to wet me once, and the wind to make me cold – when thunder would not cease at my great bidding, there I found them, there I smelt 'em out. No sirs," he looks from Edgar over to Gloucester, "they are not men of their words: they told me I was everything, but it's a lie. I am not immune to your sicknesses or your fevers after all."

"The sound of that voice I do well remember: is it not the King's?" Gloucester asks.

"Yes, every inch a king," Lear scoffs. "When I do stare, see how my subject quakes. I pardon that man's life: find this one guilty. What was your crime? Adultery?" He laughs. "You shall not die for *adultery*

– die for adultery? No! The wren goes to it, and the bluebottle breeds before my very eyes. Let copulation thrive, for Gloucester's bastard son was kinder to his father than were my daughters made between the lawful sheets of marriage. Go to it, lechery, all you desire, for I could use some soldiers." He gazes across the streambed at the fallen trees where he thinks Goneril stands staring.

"Behold yon simpering dame," he points, "whose cold looks seem to promise even colder things below, pretending delicate virtue, shaking her head at the very thought of pleasure. But nor tomcat nor stallion goes to it with more wild and wanton appetite." He whispers again. "From the waist down they are centaurs: up to the head they are all woman. Above the waist the gods possess them, beneath is all the fiend's. There's hell," he holds up one finger, "there's darkness," he puts up another, "the infernal pit, burning, scalding, stench, disease." He drops to his knees and pounds his fist on the stones. "Fie, fie, fie! *Pah, pah!* He punches harder, then sits back and looks at his hurt knuckles. "Give me a vial of musky perfume, good apothecary, to sweeten my imagination. There's money for you.."

"O, let me kiss that hand!" pleads Gloucester, holds out his arms and starts walking away.

"Let me wipe it first," Lear tells him. "It smells of mortality."

"O ruined piece of nature! Gloucester cries but trips as he turns toward the sound of Lear's voice. "This great world shall wear us down to nothing…Do you know me?" Gloucester asks.

Lear stares. "I remember your eyes, well enough. Are they winking at me?" He trudges over and sits down. "No, do your worst, pandering Cupid. I'll not love," he murmurs to himself. "Read thou this rightful claim, notice the handwriting." He points to the stones in front of Gloucester.

"Were all your letters bright as the sun, I could not see them."

"Read," Lear demands.

"With my empty sockets?"

"Ah ha! Yes," Lear nods. "Your eyes are in a dark way, your purse in a light, yet you see how this world goes."

"I feel my way."

"What, are you mad? A man may see how this world goes

without eyes. Why, look with your ears: see how yonder judge upbraids the common thief? A secret for you." He whispers to Gloucester: "Change places then choose between. Which is the judge, which the thief?" He sits back. "You've seen a dog bark at a beggar."

"I have, sir."

"And the beggar flee? There is the true meaning of authority: even a dog is obeyed when in power. You, good-for-nothing constable, remove your bloody hand! Why do you lash that whore? Flog your own back: you lust as hotly to use her in the very act for which she's being whipped. Same as the cheating judge sends the judged cheat to the gallows. In tattered clothes, small vices do appear. Robes and furred gowns can hide all: plate sin with gold, and the strongest blade of justice breaks. leaving the sinner unscathed. Arm it in rags: a pygmy's piece of straw can pierce it. No," he says, "none are guilty, none I say, none! I'll vouch for them. Take it from myself, friend, who has the power to shut the accuser's lips: get you spectacles and, like a scheming politician, make as though you understand the very things you don't." He notices Gloucester's bare feet.

"Now, now, now, now," he shakes his head in pity at the sight of the cuts and scratches. "Pull off my boots," he says and starts removing his. "Harder, harder, like so," he cries, Gloucester fumbling blindly with both of his hands in a feeble attempt to help get the boots off...

"Sense and nonsense mingled," Edgar says to himself, looking on. "Reason in madness..."

His boots off, Lear prepares to put them on Gloucester, but stops and glances up.

"If you wish to cry for your misfortunes, I'll lend you my eyes," he says quietly. "I know you well enough. Your name is Gloucester." He reaches out his hand and touches the dead black eyes. "We come crying into this world," he says gently. "The first time we smell the air, we wail and cry." He takes his hand away and studies the smear of blood on his fingers. "I will teach you then..."

"Alas, alas the day," Gloucester finds Lear's hand and kisses it.

"When we are born, we cry that we have come to this great stage of fools," Lear begins, but with a look over Gloucester's shoulder promptly breaks off: the officer and search party sent by Cordelia to find him are riding up the streambed. Lear gets to his feet, watching warily as they approach. "Remember," he whispers to Gloucester, "it were a clever trick thinking to shoe a troop of horses with felt so they could not be heard. I'll put it to the test." He steals away across the streambed. "And when I have crept up on these son-in-laws," he yells as he scrambles up the bank, "then I will *kill, kill, kill, kill, kill!*" Reaching the top, he dashes into the woods and starts running, the soldiers spurring their horses and charging up the embankment to go after him.

Their horses crashing hard through the trees, several soldiers jump down and take up the chase on foot, though Lear, with surprising speed, stays just out of reach until his feet tangle in the undergrowth: his body lurches forward and he goes down.

"Here!" A soldier yells.

"Sir, your daughter – " the officer calls, riding up and dismounting.

"No help?" Lear barks, out of breath but trying to get back on his feet. He watches as the soldiers surround him. "A prisoner," he says, when, after a final jostling cat-and-mouse around a tree, they seize him. "A natural born fool…" He looks into the faces of the young soldiers who have captured him, glances down in some confusion at the gloved hands with which they're holding him. "Treat me well. You shall have your ransom. But I will need surgeons: I am cut to the brains,"

"You shall have anything."

"No others?" Lear asks, peering around the forest, the soldiers bringing him before the officer. "By myself," he says, shakes and lowers his head despondently. "This would drive the bravest man to tears," he mutters sadly. "Water for his garden… Damp the dusty autumn road…"

"Good sir – " the officer interrupts.

Lear catches him looking at the flowers in his hair. "I will die in my wedding clothes," he responds defiantly, "like a handsome bridegroom." He stands up straight. "I am ready," he says solemnly – before jerking his arms back and breaking away. The soldiers, reacting swiftly, easily restrain him. "Come, come," he reminds them indignantly, "some majesty. I am a king. Know you not that?" he glares.

"You are a royal one, and we obey you," the officer says and bows, the other soldiers letting go of Lear to do the same.

" – With life in him yet!" he shouts jubilantly, and this time gets free. "If you want him you must catch him!" he cries, but before fleeing, jumps shrieking at the soldiers' horses to scare them away, "*Sa, sa, sa, sa!*" grabbing one by the reins, which he climbs onto, kicking it with his heels and riding off into the woods, the astounded soldiers looking sheepishly over at the officer to see what they should do.

"Hail, sir," Edgar calls from behind and comes forward holding Lear's boots.

"What's your will?" the officer grimaces, though he still has his horse.

"Do you know of the forthcoming battle, sir?"

"Certainly, sir. Anyone with ears has heard."

"But, by your favor, how near is the other army?"

"Near and coming quickly. The main force is expected at any time."

"I thank you, sir." He hands over the boots.

"Though the Queen for special reasons here remains," the officer adds as he fixes the boots to his saddle and mounts up. "Her army, however, has gone ahead."

"I thank you, sir," says Edgar, standing alone in the quiet forest once the soldiers have gone…

Gloucester is still sitting in the streambed, hands folded to pray. "You gentle gods," he starts softly, but can't find the words to continue. He sighs and waits for a moment. "You ever gentle gods," he tries again, "take my breath from me in your own time." He pauses. "Let not the evil angel that torments me, tempt me again to die before it is your will…"

"Well prayed, old man," Edgar says coming up beside him.

Gloucester nods, recognizing the voice. "But good sir," he asks earnestly, "who are you?"

Edgar thinks for a moment. "A most poor man, resigned to fortune's blows, who through lessons of pain and sorrow has learned to be generous in his pity. Give me your hand. I'll lead you to more comfortable refuge."

"Hearty thanks," he says, and with Edgar's help rises to his feet. "The bounty and blessings of heaven reward thee." Edgar crouches down so his father can climb on his back.

"A proclaimed prize!" shouts a gloating voice from the top of the embankment. Oswald has ridden up. He draws his sword and hops down from his horse. "How fortunate for me that eyeless head of yours was made to raise my fortunes!" Sliding down the bank, he strides quickly across the streambed. "You old unhappy traitor, say your prayers: the sword is ready that will destroy you." He advances, but Edgar turns so he can't get to Gloucester. Oswald goes the other way but Edgar turns too. "How dare you help a declared traitor, bold peasant? Out of the way, lest his ill fortune cost you as well. Put him down!"

"Chill not let go, zir," Edgar says in the voice of a village idiot, "without vurther 'casion."

"Let go or die, peasant!"

"Good gentleman, go your way and let poor volk pass. And chud ha' bin zwaggered out of my life, 'twould not ha bin zo long as 'tis by a vartnight. Nay, come not near the old man. Keep out, che vor ye, or I'se try whether your head be as hard as my vist, chill be plain with ye."

"Out, dunghill!" Oswald sneers and thrusts his sword at Edgar who all in one move steps away, sets down his father and scoops up a handful of stones he flings hard in Oswald's face, the sword falling from his hands when, crying out in pain, he brings them up too late to protect his eyes.

"Chill pick your teeth, zir!" Edgar cries, grabs the sword and runs Oswald through.

"Slave, thou hast slain me," he cries, his eyes blinking in disbelief at the blade sticking out of his chest. "Villain, take my purse – " he starts to say, but slumps to the ground at Edgar's feet. "If ever thou hope to thrive, bury my body, and give the letters which I have here," he pats a hand against his coat, "to Edmund Earl of Gloucester. Seek him out on the English side." His eyes roll back in his head and he dies.

"I know thee well," Edgar says and closes Oswald's eyes. "A serviceable villain as dutiful to the vices of your mistress as badness would desire."

"Is he dead?" Gloucester wonders.

"Sit you down father. Rest yourself. Let's see these pockets." He searches in Oswald's clothes and finds some folded papers. "These may be my friends. Dead," he answers Gloucester, "though I am sorry to have been his executioner. Let us see..." He takes a letter and breaks the seal. "By your leave, gentle wax, and blame not my bad manners." He opens the letter and reads: "*Let our mutual vows be remembered, you have many opportunities to be rid of him. If your desire be not lacking, time and place will amply be provided. There is no hope if he return the conqueror: then am I the prisoner still, and his bed my jail, from the loathed warmth of which, deliver me, and take his place as the reward for your great labor. Your – wife, so I would call myself – affectionate servant, and one who dares risk everything for you. Goneril.*" Edgar sits for a moment. "How boundless is a woman's lust: a plot upon her husband's life, and my brother to fill his place." He closes up the letter. "I'll bury these proofs of lechery and murder, and when the time is ripe show them to the victim Duke." He glances at Oswald. "For him, 'tis well that of your death and this scheming business I can tell..."

"The King is mad," Gloucester says, suddenly agitated. "How stubborn and shameful my reason that it keeps me standing and too feeling of my ever growing sorrows. Better I were mad myself, so should my thoughts be severed from my griefs, for woes by rapt illusion lose all knowledge of themselves..."

Edgar finishes digging a hole in the embankment but stops before he puts the letters in: he makes out the faint sound of drums in the field above. The letters buried, he covers the opening with earth and hurries back for his father.

"Come, father, take my hand. I'll bestow you with a friend." Hoisting Gloucester on his back, he crosses the streambed, clambers up the far bank and heads quickly into the woods....

Light streaming into her tent from an open flap above, Cordelia holds the chain and gold medallion sent to her during the storm, Kent looking on beside her, his appearance still disguised.

"O thou good Kent, how shall I ever repay you for your goodness? My life will be too short and every measure feel it must fall short."

"To be acknowledged, madam, is more than payment enough. The accounts I give are told in simple truth, neither more nor less."

"Don better clothes," she smiles kindly and touches the frayed arm of the coat he's wearing. These are reminders of worser times. I pray you take them off."

"Pardon, dear madam, But to make myself known at present would harm my intended plans. The reward I would ask is that I remain unknown till time and I think it proper."

"Then be it so, my good lord."

The doctor slipping quietly into the tent, she tucks the medallion away. "How does the King?"

"Sleeps still, madam."

"O you kind gods, cure this great breach in his frail and battered senses. Let him change from a child to be a man again..."

"If your Majesty please, we may wake him now: he has slept long and well."

"Be governed by your knowledge, doctor. We shall do as you see fit."

He goes to the door and calls outside.

"Stay near, good madam. I doubt not he will be in madness when we waken him."

Kent nods agreement, and turns toward the door as Cordelia's officer steps inside.

"Has he been dressed?" Cordelia asks.

"Yes, madam," the officer replies. "While in the heaviness of sleep we put fresh garments on him."

"Very well."

Lear is brought in on a litter, a soldier at each corner. The doctor points them close to Cordelia where they put the litter down, a man with a lute scurrying up to stand beside the King. He starts playing.

"If it please you, draw near," the doctor tells Cordelia. "Louder the music there," he waves to the man on the lute.

"O my dear father, healing find its medicine on my lips and let this kiss repair the horrible harm that my sisters have done to your reverence."

"A royal princess," Kent murmurs as she kisses her father.

A stool is brought and she sits down, tenderly stroking his head. " – Had you not been their father, these white strands alone would have called for their pity. Was this a face to contend against the roaring winds, resounding bolts of thunder? In the flash of terrible lightning to watch – poor lost soul – with these thin strips of hair before your blinded eyes? Mine enemy's dog, though he had bit me, would have stayed that night beside my fire. Were you glad to hovel in musty straw with madmen and vagabond rogues?" she asks, smiling down at him. "Alas, alas, 'tis a wonder your life was not ended when your wits could hold no longer. He wakes." She starts and looks to the doctor. "Speak to him."

"No, madam," the doctor says. " 'Tis best you do." He frowns at the lute player and the music stops.

Cordelia hesitates before she speaks. "How does my royal lord? How fares your Majesty?"

For a moment he continues to lie still, but then he opens his eyes and gazes up at the sunlight streaming in above her head. "You do me wrong to take me out of the grave: you are a soul in paradise, but I am bound below on a wheel of fire, my own tears scald like molten lead."

"Sir, do you know me?"

"I know you are a spirit. Where did you die?"

"Still far away…" she worries.

He sits up slowly. "Where have I been? Where am I? Fair daylight? I am confused." He looks at the faces around him. "Even I would die of pity to see another thus. I know not what to say. I will not swear these are my hands: let us see…" He pinches his hand. "I feel this." He touches his face. "Would I were sure I was not dreaming."

"O look upon me, sir" bids Cordelia. Place your hand in blessing on my head."

Lear sits forward and kneels

"You must not kneel."

"Pray, do not mock me," he looks at her. "I am a very foolish, fond old man, fourscore years and upward, not an hour more or less. And to speak plainly, I fear I am not in my right mind. Methinks I should know you." He turns to Kent. "And this man also. Yet I am doubtful, for I am entirely ignorant what place this is, and all the skill I have remembers not these clothes, nor I know not where I did lodge these nights past." Cordelia smiles. "Do not laugh at me," he tells her, and peers into her face, "for as I am a man, I think this lady to be my child Cordelia."

"And so I am, father. So I am."

"Be your tears wet?" He touches her cheek. "I think they are. I pray, weep not. If you have poison for me, I will drink it. I know you do not love me. For your sisters have, as I do remember, done me wrong. You have some cause, they have not."

"No, father, no cause."

"Am I in France?"

"In your own kingdom, sir," Kent tells him.

"Do not toy with me," he grumbles and looks away, angry.

Cordelia glances to the doctor. "Rest easy, good madam: the great rage in him is done, yet it would be dangerous to make him more mindful of the time he has been lost."

"Will it please you to be alone?" Cordelia asks her father.

He meets her eyes. "Pray you now, forgive me. I am old and foolish…"

The doctor signals for all to leave, only Cordelia remaining behind…

Outside the tent, the officer takes Kent aside. "Is it true the Duke of Cornwall has been slain?"

"Most true, sir."

"Who has command of his people?"

"The bastard son of Gloucester, or so 'tis said."

"They say Edgar, the banished son, is with the Earl of Kent in Germany."

"Put little stock in rumors, sir. 'Tis time to look to it, the armies of the kingdom are approaching."

"The action is like to be fierce," the officer says and slips on his gloves. "Fare you well, sir."

Kent watches him go, columns of uniformed soldiers marching past the tent on their way out of camp. "The purposed aim and object of my life," he says quietly to himself, "for good or ill, will come amid this battle's bloody strife…."

The blue waters of the English Channel visible in the distance, the British have made their camp on a hill overlooking the wide, sloping field where the battle with the French and those supporting Lear will take place. Edmund, dressed for battle, and Regan, wearing light armor, are sitting on their horses out front of the camp as the signal drums sound the call to arms: grim-faced soldiers with swords and shields, armor-clad horsemen clutching axes and spears, hurry to take their positions along the broad crest of the hill.

Edmund motions to an officer nearby who comes over. "Find out if the Duke is still intending to fight, or whether he's changed his mind." The officer bows and rides off. "Bring me a decision quickly!" Edmund calls after him.

Regan looks over. "Our sister's steward has surely come to harm," she says, but without concern.

"I fear it's so, madam."

She musters the courage to speak. "You know the goodness I intend upon you, my lord," she says eagerly. "Tell me, but truly, and only speak the truth, do you not love my sister?"

"In honorable love I do," he says.

"But have you never found a husband's way," she pauses, "to the forbidden place?"

He throws her a chiding glance. "That thought is most unworthy of you, madam."

"I fear you have been with her. Enjoyed her private touch."

"No, by my honor, madam, I have not."

"I cannot stand her," Regan bursts in anger. "Dear my lord, be not familiar with her," she pleads.

"Doubt me not," he tells her and points. "She and the Duke her husband…"

Albany and Goneril, on their horses, are approaching.

"I had rather lose the battle than lose him to my sister," Goneril murmurs with a glare at Regan.

"Our very loving sister, welcome," Albany says, greeting Goneril. He turns to Edmund. "Sir, I have heard the King is now with his daughter and others whom the harshness of recent measures has forced into rebellion." He stares coldly. "Where I cannot be honorable, I never yet could be brave: as for this business, it concerns us only so far as France invades our land, not because he backs the King and those demanding justice."

"Sir, you speak nobly."

"Why is this being discussed?" Regan demands, annoyed.

"You are together against the enemy," Goneril adds sharply. "These proud disputes are not the question here."

Albany nods and lets things pass. "Let's gather with our captains then, and determine our proceeding."

"I shall attend you presently at your tent," Edmund says and turns his horse to go.

Regan moves to follow him, but stops and looks at Goneril. "Sister, you'll go with us?"

"No."

"It is fitting that you should," Regan says. "Pray, go with us."

"I know the reason she would ask this," Goneril says, a bitter smile for her sister. "I will go then," she changes her mind and heads with them over to the tents.

"If ever your grace had speech with man so poor, let me have a word."

Edgar has come to stand a short distance away.

"Speak," Albany orders.

Stepping forward, Edgar hands a letter up to him.

"Before you begin the battle, sir, open this letter. If you are victorious, let the trumpet sound to summon him who brought it.

Lowly as I seem, I can produce a noble warrior who will prove what's here maintained. If you are defeated, your business in this world is done with, and plotted intrigue ceases. May fortune favor you…"

"Stay till I read the letter," Albany calls as Edgar walks away.

He stops and turns. "I was forbid that. When the time is ripe let the trumpet sound and I'll appear again."

"Fare you well then. I'll look it over." He peers at the name on the letter, but when he glances up, Edgar has disappeared.

"The enemy's in sight," Edmund announces, riding up. "Form your lines." He holds some papers out to Albany. "Here are their numbers and deployment, gathered by my spies – haste is urged upon you, my lord."

Albany snatches the papers without looking at Edmund. "We'll meet the appointed time," he says coldly, spurs his horse and gallops off to take command of his troops.

The papers thrown to the ground, Edmund dismounts and walks over to retrieve them. "To both these sisters have I sworn my love," he muses idly, "each sister jealous of the other as those by adders stung." He gazes toward the battlefield. "Which of them shall I take? Both? One? Or neither? Neither can be enjoyed if both remain alive," he reasons. "To take the widow makes mad her sister Goneril, but hardly can I keep my loving bargain, her husband being alive…" He tucks the papers inside his belt and climbs back on his horse. "We'll use his grave authority in the battle," he smiles, "which being done, let Goneril, who would be rid of him, devise his speedy taking off. The mercy which he has in mind for Lear and for Cordelia, the battle won, and they within our power, shall never see his pardon: my fortunes depend on me to finish this fight, not argue and dispute over what is wrong or right…"

Carrying Gloucester on his back, Edgar moves through the woods alongside the battlefield where the fighting is heated and fierce: drums beating, swords and axes clashing, men and horses cut and bleeding fall amid the din of vicious battle.

"Here, old father, stay behind this tree and wait for him who is coming for you. Pray the side of right may thrive. If ever we two meet again, I'll bring you joyful news."

Gloucester reaches out for Edgar's hands and takes them in his own. "Grace go with you, sir."

Edgar runs out from the trees and onto the field where all is havoc and chaos. An English horse thunders by, the rider swinging his axe and severing a French man's arm from his shoulder. A French soldier fights a British man to the ground but doesn't see another run up behind him until it's too late: his throat has been slit and the knife plunged through his chest before he has time to cry out. Edgar races back to the forest.

"Away, old man!" he calls when he returns to Gloucester by his tree. "Give me your hand. Away!" He tries to get Gloucester on his feet, but the old man refuses to budge. "King Lear has lost," Edgar tells him. "He and his daughter captured! Give me thy hand," he urges. "Come!"

"No further, sir. A man may die here as well as anywhere."

"What, dark thoughts again?" Edgar asks. "We must endure the leaving of this world," he says to his father, "even as our coming to it: readiness is all."

Gloucester stays sitting down, thinking of what's been said. Edgar, beside him, worries that time is running short: the battle is spreading into the woods, where the retreating French are fleeing the butchery on the field.

"Perhaps this is true," Gloucester finally says and struggles to his feet....

...With the battle won, wounded British soldiers are hobbling into camp, making way for the wagons that are heading out to collect the dead on the battlefield. Guards are watching over their glum French prisoners, seated on the ground, arms on their knees, their heads bowed in defeat, while close by, Lear and Cordelia, their wrists tied with rope, are brought before Edmund.

"Some officers take them away," he commands. "Keep them under close guard until it is decided what to do with them."

"We are not the first with best intentions who have incurred the worst," Cordelia. ventures to her father. "For you, oppressed King, I am cast down, myself could otherwise smile that Fortune has not favored us today." She looks to Edmund. "Shall we not see these daughters who are my sisters?" she asks him, but busy with one of his officers, he doesn't give an answer.

Lear turns her away from him. "No, no, no, no! Come, let's away to prison," he says with a cheery smile. "We two alone will sing like birds in the cage. When thou dost ask my blessing, I'll kneel down and ask of thee forgiveness. So we'll live. And pray, and sing, and tell old tales, and laugh at mincing courtiers, and hear poor rogues as they rave and rant about the news in higher quarters. And we'll talk with them too: who loses, who wins, who's in, who's out, and ponder the mysteries of life as if the gods had let us spy into their secrets... And we'll pass the time in a walled prison, watching great ones come and go, their fortunes ever changing like the tides that ebb and flow."

"Take them away," Edmund calls to the guards.

"The gods will bless and celebrate our sacrifice, Cordelia. Don't you see? Only the heavens could ever part us, you and I. Wipe thine eyes. What goes around shall come around, devouring these enemies before they'll make us weep. We'll see 'em starved first. Come..."

Edmund catches the eye of an officer and draws him aside. "Take you this note and follow them to prison. Promotion to the highest rank awaits thee. If you do as this instructs you, you'll make your way to noble fortune. Know this too: men are as the times in which they live. To be tenderhearted does not become a soldier. This great task needs no chewing over. Either you'll do it, or henceforth make your way by other means."

The officer meets Edmund's eyes. "I'll do it, my lord," he nods.

"About it then, and write saying 'success' when it is done. Remember, I say instantly. Carry it out exactly as I've set it down."

"I cannot pull a cart, nor do I eat dried oats," the officer boasts simply, "but if it be a man's work, I'm the man to do it."

He goes, passing Albany, Goneril and Regan who are riding out from the camp to greet Edmund now that the battle is over. They get down from their horses and come over, Goneril looking away as Regan embraces him.

"Sir," Albany offers, "you have shown today your valiant side, and fortune led you well. I believe you have the captives who opposed us in this strife. I do require them of you, so to treat them as they are deserving and as our safety may determine."

"Sir, I thought it fit to send the old and miserable King to his confinement under quick and heavy guard, his age brings sympathy with it, his title more. These could pluck the hearts of people, turn them mightily against us. With him I sent the Queen, my reason just the same, they are ready later or tomorrow to appear where you shall hold your trial. Now we sweat and bleed: friend has lost friend, and before the heat of the fray has cooled, the best of causes are cursed by those who've had to endure the pain of brutal battle. The question of Cordelia and her father requires a fitter time and place."

"Sir, so that you know, I hold you as a subject, not a brother in this war."

"That's as I choose to honor him," Regan objects. "Methinks my wishes might have been asked for ere you went so far," she glares at Albany. "He led my troops, bore the commission of my place and person, in which regard he may stand up and call you royal brother before too long."

Goneril is livid. "In his own right he has proved himself, aside from any honors you bestow."

"But with the rights conferred by me, he stands among the best."

"And what of the right to husband him?" Albany pointedly puts in.

"Many a truth is spoke in jest," Regan comes back, but winces from a pain in her stomach.

"No sister," Goneril sneers. "Your jealous eyes deceive you."

"Lady, I am not well, otherwise I would answer this in anger. She looks to Edmund. "General, take you my soldiers, prisoners, inheritance, rights and all, take charge of them, of me. All I have is yours. Let the world witness that I create thee here my lord and master."

"Mean you to sleep with him?" Goneril sneers coldly.

"The power to prevent which lies not in your permission," Albany upbraids her.

"Nor in yours either," Edmund says.

"True, bastard fellow."

"Let the drum strike, and combat prove my titles are yours," Regan declares, hearing Edmund so insulted.

"Hold. Hear reason," Albany commands and turns. "Edmund, I arrest thee on capital treason, and thy partner in conspiracy, this smiling serpent here," he glares at Goneril, then back at Regan. "For your claim, sister, I bar it on behalf of my wife. 'Tis she is pledged to this lord, and I, her husband, forbid your marriage on her behalf. If you will marry, make your overtures to me: my lady is spoken for."

"How pitiful these dramatics," Goneril scoffs, but Albany simply ignores her.

"You are armed, Gloucester. Let the trumpet sound. If none appear to prove thy many heinous treasons," he takes off and throws down his glove, "*there* is my challenge. I'll prove it to be true thou art no less guilty than I have here proclaimed thee."

"Sick," Regan cries, dizzily reeling, "I am sick…"

"If not, I'll n'er trust poison again," mutters Goneril.

Edmund removes his glove and throws it down before Albany. "There is mine to challenge you, lord. "Whoever he is who calls me traitor, lies like a villain. Sound the trumpet. He that dares approach, to him, to you – to anyone!" he shouts across the field, "will I maintain my truth and honor firmly."

"A herald then!" Albany calls. "And lord, it is up to your own courage now, for your soldiers, all enlisted in my name, have in my name now been discharged."

"My sickness grows upon me!"

"She is not well," says Albany. "Convey her to my tent." Guards rush forward and take Regan away, Albany turning to the herald who has come forward with his horn. "Let the trumpet sound and read out this." He hands him the letter Edgar gave him before the battle.

The herald blows his trumpet, then lowers it and opens the letter to read. " 'If any man of quality or rank within the army lists, will maintain upon Edmund, supposed Duke of Gloucester, that he is a manifold traitor, let him appear by the third sound of the trumpet. He is bold in his defense.' "

"Sound!" cries Edmund.

The herald blows again, then twice more, but another trumpet sounds nearby, a second herald leading a man in armor forward, his head covered in a dark iron helmet with small holes at the eyes, the nose and mouth.

"Ask him his purposes!" shouts Albany. "Why he appears upon this call of the trumpet."

"What are you?" the herald turns and demands. "Your name, your rank, and why you answer this present summons."

"Know this," says Edgar. "My name is lost. By treason's tooth gnawed bare and badly bit, I yet am noble as the adversary I come to face."

"Which is that adversary?"

"He that calls himself Edmund, Earl of Gloucester."

"I am that man," Edmund declares and steps forward. "What say'st thou to him?"

"Draw thy sword," Edgar says. "And if my speech offend you, your arm may do you justice and put me in my proper place. Here is mine." He takes out his sword and begins walking toward Edmund. "Behold, it is my privilege, the privilege of my knighted ranks, the oath of my profession, to have this challenge met." He stops walking. "Despite your younger strength, your rank and noble standing, your triumph in the battle and your newfound royal titles, I declare you are a traitor, false to your gods, your brother and your father – conspirator against this high illustrious prince of Albany, and from the top of your vile head to the dust beneath your feet, a wretched and worthless traitor. Say you 'no'? This sword, this arm and my most noble valor, are with all my heart determined now to prove you lie."

"In wisdom I should ask your name, but since your outside looks so fair and warlike, your voice some signs of breeding breathes, what scruple and what caution would expect me to disdain and spurn, by all the rules of knighthood, I toss these treasons back at you. But as I know that way they do no harm, I'll drive these hateful lies into your heart upon my sword, where they shall rest forever. Trumpet, speak!"

Both heralds raise their horns and signal combat.

Edmund strikes fast and hard, but Edgar holds his own, deflecting his brother's punishing blows and not attempting to swing with any himself. On they fight, grunting and wrestling, with Edgar unwilling to strike – until his brother, panting, is suddenly slow in raising his sword. Edgar lunges swiftly and plants his blade hard in Edmund's side. His face surprised despite his wound, he frowns briefly then falls to the ground, Edgar above him instantly, sword poised to render the finishing blow.

"Let him live!" Albany calls behind them.

"This is treachery, Glouccstcr!" Goneril cries. "By the laws of war you were not obliged to answer this unknown man. You are not vanquished, but cheated and deceived!"

"Shut your mouth, woman," Albany tells her. "Or with this letter I will shut it for you. Hold, sir!" he calls to Edgar, showing Goneril the letter he was given. "Thou worse than any name, read thine own evil." She glares at the letter in front of her then grabs for it. "No tearing, lady. Clearly you know it."

"And what if I do? The laws are mine, not thine: who can indict me for it?"

"You are more than monstrous, you," Albany sneers, disgusted. "Do you know this letter?"

"Ask me not what I know." She stalks back to her horse, climbs on and rides into the camp.

"Go after her," Albany orders. "She's desperate. Take charge of her." An officer and soldiers mount up and ride off.

"What you have charged me with, I have done," Edmund says to his brother. "And more, much more. In time it will come out. 'Tis over and done with, and so am I." He winces with the pain of his bleeding wound. "But who are you that has defeated me? If you are noble, I forgive thee."

"My forgiveness and love to you as well. I am no less in blood than thou art, Edmund. If greater as the legitimate, the greater you have wronged me. My name is Edgar, your father's son." He removes his helmet. "The gods are just, and of our pleasure-seeking vices make instruments to plague us. The dark and shameful lover's bed wherein you were created, has cost a man his blessed eyes."

"Thou hast spoken right, 'tis true. The wheel has come full circle. I am here..."

"It seemed your self conveyed a royal nobleness," says Albany. "I must embrace thee. Let sorrow break my heart if ever I did hate thee or thy father."

"Worthy prince, it is no matter now."

"Where have you hidden yourself? How come to know the miseries of your father?"

"I took care of him, my lord. If you will hear, and my heart not break in telling, the tale is this: to escape the proclamation condemning me to death – how sweet is life that we can bear the constant fear of death when a single stroke might end our terror – I changed into a madman's rags, taking on the semblance of a beggar that even dogs disdained wherever I did wander. While in this guise I met my father soon after his precious eyes were lost, their sockets but bleeding holes. Became his guide, led him, begged for him, saved him from his despair. Never – O sad mistake – revealed myself to him until a half-hour past, when came I armed to you, not sure, though hoping for success. I asked his blessing, and first to last described the journey we had made together. But his broken heart – alas, too weak to bear the shock – between extremes of passion, joy and grief, burst happily and he died."

"These words of yours have moved me," Edmund groans, "and perhaps can do some good. – Continue on, you look as if there's something more you wish to say."

"If there be more, more woeful than this, hold it in, for I feel my tears about to break," Albany says, shaken.

"Sadly I say there is, my lord. While I was grieving loudly for my father's death, there came a man who glimpsed me in my sorrowful weeping state, but passed me by as one like all the others hurt and dying after the battle. I called to him and, finding who it was that so endured, he fastened his arms around my neck and bellowed out in anguish, threw himself upon my father next and told the most piteous tale of him and Lear that ears have ever heard. His grief so overwhelming, the strings of life began to crack – twice then the trumpets sounded and there I left him, feinted beside my father."

"Help, help, O help!" a soldier shrieks, rides in and jumps from his horse.

"What? What?" Edgar demands.

"Speak man," Albany tells him. The soldier holds up a knife, dripping with blood.

"What means this?"

" 'Tis hot. It steams. It came from her heart just now," he cries. "O, she's dead," he wails.

"Who's dead? Speak man!" Albany shouts.

"Your lady, sir, your lady. And her sister by her is poisoned. She confesses it."

Hearing the news, Edmund tries to sit up. "I was betrothed to both of them," He says, staring off. "Three sisters dead together…"

"Kent comes," Edgar informs Albany.

"Bring out their bodies, alive or dead," Albany tells the soldier, who leaves the knife and goes. "This judgment of the heavens that makes us tremble, troubles us not," he says of his wife and Regan, and watches Kent approach. "Is this he? Time will not allow us to welcome him as we should," he offers gravely.

"I am come to bid my king and master forever good night," Kent lets them know upon arriving. He peers around, surprised. "But is he not here?"

"Great matter by us forgot!" Albany cries. ""Speak, Edmund, where's the King? And Cordelia?"

The bodies of Regan and Goneril are brought out from the camp, draped over the backs of their horses. Several soldiers lift them off and lay them on the ground.

"See'st thou this spectacle, Kent?"

"Alas, why thus?"

"In spite of all," Edmund says, struggling to speak, "I was beloved of them both." The one the other poisoned for my sake, and after, killed herself." He gasps for breath, beckoning Edgar over. "Some good I mean to do, against my despised nature. Quickly send, quickly," he says weakly, "to the prison. My order's given on the life of Lear and Cordelia. Go, send in time!"

"Run, O run!" Albany orders his guards.

"To *who*, my lord?" Edgar demands and lifts his brother's head. "*Who* has the order? What sign of reprieve would serve?"

Edmund pats the ground beside him. "Take my sword. To the captain – "

Edgar finds the sword and runs it over to a soldier already on his horse. "Haste thee, for thy life." The soldier charges off.

" – His orders," Edmund falters to Albany, "from thy wife and me…were to hang Cordelia in the prison…then lay the blame on her own despair…that she had killed herself."

"The gods defend her! Take him away for now," Albany says, repulsed.

"Howl, howl, howl, howl!" Lear's harrowing voice goes up close by on the field of battle. He makes his way forward, staggering between dead and dying bodies of soldiers both French and English that are strewn across the field, Cordelia in his arms, a noose around her neck. "You are men of stone!" he bellows. "Had I your tongues and eyes, I'd hurl them at the heavens. She's gone forever. I know when one is dead and when one lives. She's dead as earth." He lays the body down and kneels beside it. "Lend me a looking-glass. If that her breath will mist or stain it, why then she lives."

"Is this the end of days?" Kent says in misery.

"Or image of its doom…" Edgar can only stare.

"Let the heavens fall into the sun," Albany moans.

Lear crawls on the ground until he finds something. He holds it above Cordelia's face. "This feather stirs! She lives! If it be so, it is a boon which does redeem all sorrows that I've ever felt."

"O my good master," says Kent, stepping closer.

"No, away," Lear tells him.

" 'Tis noble Kent, your friend," Edgar offers.

"A plague upon you, murderers, traitors all! I might have saved her. Now she's gone forever. Cordelia, Cordelia, stay a little." Sobbing, he lays his head on her chest. "What's that you say?" he sits up. "Her voice was ever soft, gentle and low," he gazes down. "Like her mother's… I killed the slave who hanged thee," he sneers. "Did I not fellow?" A soldier who has followed him nods to Albany and the others. "I have seen the day, with my good biting falcon, I would have made them jump!" He heaves a sigh. "I am old now. The troubles of age have dampened me. Who are you?" he notices Kent. "Mine eyes are not the best." He stands up and goes closer. "I'll tell you in a moment." He stops walking and peers at Kent's bloody and char-smudged face. "This is a sad sight. Are you not Kent?"

"The same, your servant Kent. Where is your servant Caius, who walked with you?"

"He's a good fellow, I can tell you that," Lear allows himself a smile. "He'll strike, and quickly too. He's dead and rotten."

"No, my good lord, I am the very man."

Lear looks away absently. "I'll see to that hereafter," he mutters, shaking his head as he remembers his faithful servant.

"I am he that from the start of your decline has followed your sad steps," Kent continues.

But Lear is lost in thought. "You are welcome hither," he murmurs quietly."

Kent shakes his head. "None are, sir. All's cheerless, dark and deadly. Your eldest daughters have destroyed themselves and in despair are dead."

"So I gather," Lear says and casts his eyes at the bodies of Regan and Goneril.

"He knows not what he says, Albany points out. "It is unwise we tell him too much all at once."

"It avails nothing," Edgar agrees.

"Edmund is dead, my lords," a soldier arrives and announces.

"That is but a trifle here." Albany turns to his captains and commanders who have gathered in the field around him. "You lords and noble friends, know our fast intent. All comfort to this great but ruined man shall be afforded. As for us, we will restore, during the life of this old Majesty, to him his absolute power. To you," he looks to Kent and Edgar, "your rights and titles, and such others as your honors more than merit. All friends shall taste the wages of their virtue, and all our foes the cup of fair deserving. O look. Look!"

Lear has put his arms under Cordelia and is feebly trying to lift her. "And my poor fool is hanged – no, no, no life?" he asks Edgar who kneels and settles him down, and cradling Lear's head in his arms. "Why should a dog, a horse, a rat, have life, and thou no breath at all? Thou'lt come no more," he looks to Cordelia. "Never, never, never, never, never..." He stays quiet a long moment. "Pray you," he touches his throat, "undo this button." Edgar loosens the collar of his shirt. "Thank you, sir," he says gratefully. He turns his head so he can see Cordelia. "Do you see this? Look there, look there," he says, and lifts his hand to point, but his eyes close, his mouth falls open, and he dies...

"Break heart," Kent whispers. "I pray thee break."

"Look up my lord," Edgar pleads.

"Vex not his ghost," says Kent. "He hates him that on the rack of this tough world would stretch him any longer. The wonder is he hath endured so long. He but outlived his time."

"Bear them from here," Albany says solemnly. "Our present business is general mourning. Friends of my soul," he says to Kent and Edgar, "you twain rule in this realm and our gored state sustain."

Kent shakes his head. "I have a journey, sir, shortly to go. My master calls me, I must not say no."

Edgar lays Lear beside Cordelia and gets to his feet. "The weight of this sad time we must obey," he declares for all to hear. "Speak what we feel, not what we ought to say. The oldest hath borne most: we that are young shall never see so much, nor live so long."

He turns to speak with Kent, but Lear's true and faithful friend has left without bidding adieu, to shape his old course in a country new....

New Directions

The Young and the Restless: *Change*

The Human Season: *Time and Nature*

Eyes Wide Shut: *Vision and Blindness*

Cosmos: *The Light and The Dark*

Nothing But: *The Truth in Shakespeare*

Relationscripts: *Characters as People*

Idol Gossip: *Rumours and Realities*

Wherefore?? *The Why in Shakespeare*

Upstage, Downstage: *The Play's the Thing*

Being There: *Exteriors and Interiors*

Dangerous Liaisons: *Love, Lust and Passion*

Iambic Rap: *Shakespeare's Words*

P.D.Q.: *Problems, Decisions, Quandaries*

Antic Dispositions: *Roles and Masks*

The View From Here: *Public vs. Private Parts*

3D: *Dreams, Destiny, Desires*

Mind Games: *The Social Seen*

Vox: *The Voice of Reason*

The Shakespeare Novels

Spring 2006

Hamlet
King Lear
Macbeth
Midsummer Night's Dream
Othello
Romeo and Juliet
Twelfth Night

Spring 2007

As You Like It
Measure for Measure
The Merchant of Venice
Much Ado About Nothing
The Taming of the Shrew
The Tempest

www.crebermonde.com

Shakespeare Graphic Novels

Fall 2006

Hamlet
Macbeth
Othello
Romeo and Juliet

www.shakespearegraphic.com

Paul Illidge is a novelist and screenwriter who taught high school English for many years. He is the creator of *Shakespeare Manga*, the plays in graphic novel format, and author of the forthcoming *Shakespeare and I*. He is currently working on *Shakespeare in America*, a feature-film documentary. Paul Illidge lives with his three children beside the Rouge River in eastern Toronto.